Grinding My Gears

An (Off-The-Rails) Ice Era Chronicle

1:30 a.m.

By C.M. Moore

www.trollriverpub.com
Grinding My Gears
An (Off-the-Rails) Ice Era Chronicle: 1:30 a.m.
Copyright © 2017 C.M. Moore
ISBN: 978-1-946454-26-3

Join the fun with Author C.M. Moore for giveaways, updates and new release opportunities at: http://eepurl.com/dnoLrr

Dear Readers,

I'm writing a little note to you about my Off-The-Rails books, but as always, I'm a slow burn. I'll get to that. I promise. Stay with me.

When I first started writing books, it was simply a hobby with my wife Monica. Monica and I would sit across from each other at our favorite café and create. We'd laugh about our characters, we'd play God and toss problems their way, and mostly I loved the way her eyes would shine when a great idea would slip from her lips.

Nothing about that has changed. This is still our hobby, our love affair. I still sit with her and the books can only be created with her at my side. However, as I started to get drawn deeper into this world of ice and snow, I began to learn more about myself. I think that anyone who writes knows that somewhere along the way we can't help but pour out a little of our soul when we tell a story.

And so, the birth of the Off-The-Rails.

Off-The-Rails stories are not only male/female love stories. They can be gay, bisexual, a mix-and-match. In short… different. Things I'm exploring about myself. Things I'm exploring about life. I write these as my own experimental contemplations as well as painting a futuristic landscape that isn't black and white.

Today we live in a world as varied as a rainbow flag, different in ideas, as sexual preference, as in skin color. And since this series of books is set in the future, I can't imagine a world that doesn't still have gay couples, lesbians, or threesomes. To be honest, I don't want a place where these mixes and matches are missing. It would be gray. Diversity adds color.

My Off-The-Rails stories are partly here as companion novels to the times. They add range. I will never tell my fictional characters who to love anymore then I would tell someone on the street who they should be with. These stories may upset your moral compass a bit, but I promise you, I'm writing the correct story for the character at hand. This is their world, their journey, as much as it is mine.

But in case you're not a fan of the Off-The-Rails, don't be worried. 1:05 a.m., 2:05 a.m., 3:05 a.m. etc. will always stay male/female for those who prefer it. I get that sometimes that's just want you want to read. No one will ever have to read the Off-The-Rails to understand the main story line. Without reading the other books you will be able to follow me as we march closer to whether Earth turns into a ball of ice floating in the universe… or warming up the planet somehow and everyone surviving. The books with the time titles will always be the ones where Monica and I move the Ice Era along, but the Off-The-Rails will have their place too. I hope you're cool with that.

Warm regards,

Connor & Monica Moore

~C.M.~

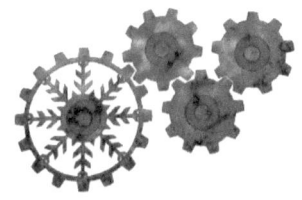

The wound is the place where the Light enters you.~ Rumi

Chapter 1

"Love is the bridge between you and everything." ~ Rumi

There were a lot of things he could handle, but congestive heart failure wasn't one of them. Especially since it was *his* heart that had decided it didn't want to beat anymore. For the first time in his life, Gears didn't have any answers.

"Doctor Gears… I hate to tell you this, but…" The doctor hesitated. Gears recognized that hesitation. That was the same pause he used when giving bad news.

"Just call me Gears," he said to fill the silence of the other doctor's exam room. He wished he was anywhere but here.

"It's getting worse. What you've been doing hasn't resulted in the improvements you'd hoped for." Doctor Dana picked up a neat stack of medical documents off his desk. Gears' name and information were printed in bold lettering on the top of the first page.

Gears didn't respond. Instead, he decided to get dressed. After pulling his sweater over his head, he picked up his thick coat while he shoved all his emotions down. He'd never really gotten the knack of dealing with turbulent feelings. He preferred logic, levelheadedness, and practicality. He ruthlessly sucked down the fear and panic. All he needed to do was… nothing came to him. He didn't know what to say or do. He was dying. Dana hadn't said that, but that was what he meant.

"I'm planning on going to H.S.P.C. Headquarters in Dallas." Gears tugged on his long, tan down coat as he slid off the sterile metal table. "This information won't change that."

"I think that's a good decision. I'll be there to help you."

"I don't need anyone. I'm a doctor." He snapped at the other man as he snapped his coat closed.

Dana looked momentarily taken aback, then he nodded. Gears thought briefly about apologizing. He was frustrated at life right now, not at the new doctor. This was it. There was nothing more they could do. He couldn't accept that. He refused. There had to be an answer somewhere. Picking up his black backpack from the floor, he swung the bag onto his back. He would figure out this puzzle by himself. He could do it. In the past, he'd always solved problems like this on his own.

"I'm sorry. I think I'll go." Gears took two steps toward the exit.

"Before you go, I want to say something. I plan to stay for the birth of Karma's baby. That was the agreement I made with Keith. I think with the two of us, and the midwife, it should go smoothly." Dana glanced down at the papers in his hands then held them out for Gears to take. "But I think that before I leave the base, you should tell Karma and Mac." He paused again. "Specifically, Mac."

Gears snatched the papers out of the other man's hand. He stuffed them into his bag. He wasn't going to tell his friend. He wasn't going to tell anyone. Even though lying went against his private code of honor, Gears had chosen to keep this a secret from both Karma and Mac. He'd told them that he was just going to Headquarters to work on information the C.T.O.N.A. had released about Snow Flu. It wasn't an outright lie, but that didn't give him peace. True, he was going to do as much as he could for the growing population who were sick, but he was really going to get access to better medical care. Telling all this to Mac would only bring around pity and coddling. Gears wasn't going to leave as a dying man, and he wasn't going to heap his problems on his best friend, particularly not when he had a new baby due any day. He was alright on his own. He was, after all, a brilliant scientist.

Returning to the door, Gears rested his hand on the knob.

"Keith asked you to come here because he was concerned about Karma giving birth with only a male doctor, and he misunderstood your name. If you hadn't shown up, no one would know about me. I plan to keep this between us. I expect you to honor doctor-patient confidentiality." Gears didn't turn around but stubbornly stared forward. He was acting as wooden as the door, but he didn't care.

"Is that the polite way of telling me to butt out?"

Gears glanced over his shoulder. "I didn't think I was being polite."

"I respect your wishes even if I don't agree with them. I want you to know that I plan to travel with you to Dallas when you're ready to relocate. We may not get along very well, Doctor, but you're my patient whether you like it or not."

Gears' shoulders slumped. This conversation was exhausting. He didn't want to have a doctor taking care of him. He hated lying to his best friend. And most of all, he didn't want to be dying because his heart was pumping incorrectly.

Taking one last look over his shoulder, he nodded to Dana. "Good afternoon, Doctor."

"Good afternoon."

The words were barely out of Doctor Dana's mouth when there was a loud rap that grabbed their attention.

"Doctor? Oye?" The words were followed by more banging. Gears threw open the door. Essie was standing on the other side. The tall Hispanic water base guard had his black curly hair sticking up everywhere. Sweat dotted the young man's brow. He looked like he'd run through the base.

"Gears!" Essie exclaimed. "Karma's having her baby. Boss sent me to get you."

"She's two days early," Dana commented as he picked up a large green medical case off his desk.

"She's in her room with Mac." Essie was breathing hard. Another indication that he might've run through the base. Either that or a signifier that he should quit smoking. "I've been looking for you."

"We're coming right now." Gears pushed everything Doctor Dana had just told him about his heart out of his mind. Mac's baby was more important. The child would be his only focus right now. Whenever anything was too scary to deal with, he took solace in his work. He was absolutely going to do that now.

"You go ahead of us, Essie." Dana waited for Gears in the water base hall. "Tell Mac to check her contractions like Doctor Gears taught him. Make her comfortable."

"Did you tell the midwife?" Gears asked as Dana closed the door behind them. They started down the hall. "Keith wanted a woman there."

"I'll do that next." Essie was off like a shot. Gears glanced to the other doctor when he put his hand out to stop Gears from chasing after the twenty-year-old.

"You're not running anywhere," Dana frowned. "You'll walk. Slowly."

So much for being able to ignore his failing heart.

Chapter 2

"Lovers don't finally meet somewhere. They're in each other all the time." Rumi~

"One more push, Karma." Gears spoke in an even voice. He had no idea if she needed to push one more time or not. She might have to push half a dozen more times, but he couldn't very well say that. Mac was on her left and their hands were wound together. Her knuckles were white. His friend nodded.

"Damn," Karma grunted. Dana, who stood on her right, patted her forehead with a cold cloth. Gears had the feeling that Dana was there more to keep an eye on him than to help with the birth. Both of them knew that Karma was completely healthy, and there were no complications. She didn't need two doctors and a midwife. Just the midwife might've been enough. Of course, Mac had insisted that Gears deliver his child.

Karma huffed, then tipped forward at an angle on the birthing chair the midwife had insisted on. Between her legs, the baby's head crowned. Carefully, he supported the fragile form. He'd never delivered a baby before. For a second, he prayed to God that he was doing it right. Sweat rolled between his shoulder blades. His heart was pounding. He needed to slow his heartbeat.

His eyes flipped to the midwife who hovered at his elbow. She smiled at him and nodded before urging Karma to breathe. All the books he'd read on this subject became silent in his head. Blood and fluids coated his hands. The baby's soft, slippery form slid from Karma's body. With one last muttered swear word, the tiny life was in his arms.

Quickly, he made sure the baby was breathing. Soon the child's cry replaced his mother's curses. He could feel everyone's eyes on him.

"Is everything okay?" Mac asked. His eyes jumped back and forth from Gears to the midwife, Aiko. Mac's eyes landed on Gears' face. "You look worried."

"You have a perfect baby boy," he replied as he tried to take a relaxing breath. His heart was pounding. Gears was confident he'd said the right thing because Mac visibly relaxed. His shoulders dropped, then a broad smile spread on his lips.

Gears looked down at the child again. Life was hard. God was merciful to have given this boy parents like Karma and Mac. When he looked back up, Mac was wrapping his arms around his wife. She reached out for the baby. Gears placed the child in her arms, and while she held him, Gears showed his friend where to cut the umbilical cord.

In a daze, Gears got up from the stool at her feet. As water base doctor, he'd closed hundreds of wounds and helped with multiple injuries, but he had never done anything like this before. He turned to Aiko, the midwife Keith had sent for when he found out that Dana wasn't a woman.

"We have to clean the baby. Cleanliness is next to godliness." He pushed up his glasses.

Aiko gave a chuckle. "The mother and child are bonding, but yes, we can do that next. You did pretty well for your first time, but you look pale."

"I'll get the towels." Gears struggled to put one foot in front of the other. He walked around to check on the baby. Karma had instantly started to nurse. He wasn't sure if he should stop her, but the midwife seemed completely accepting of her actions, and so did Dana. How Karma could stand the mess was beyond him, but then again, maybe when it was your child you felt different about being covered in blood and mucus.

"I have everything set." Gears reached the counter on the far wall and leaned heavily against the side. He paused, hoping no one noticed how wobbly he was. The other doctor's eyes had caught his before he took Gears' vacated spot to handle the evacuation of the placenta.

"Come on, little man, you're yucky." Mac pulled the little tike from his mother's arms and handed him to Gears without question. Gears was struck anew at how fragile the boy was. This must be what it was like to hold a live bomb.

"Yucky. That's a fancy medical term." Gears smiled at Mac. He held the child in his arms, pulling him close to his chest uncaring of the disgusting bodily fluids after all. He made sure not to say "disgusting" out loud. Mac might find the word funny, but Karma wouldn't. Already she was glaring at them for saying "yucky". He wrinkled his nose at the baby. Mac's boy was ugly, but in a magnificent, raw sort of way.

Gears began to gently wipe the baby clean with a soft cloth. The coppery smell of blood invaded his nostrils. All of a sudden, everything he'd learned from the midwife and the books came back to him in a rush. He glanced behind him at the group standing in Mac's apartment. Dana was giving Mac advice about the aftercare of his wife. Aiko's dark head was bent while she helped Karma off the birthing chair.

"What're you going to name him?" Aiko asked while she helped Karma into a bed near the corner.

Gears turned to face the two women with the baby bundled in his arms. He walked over to Karma and gradually handed her boy back to her. His eyes shifted around Karma and Mac's main living room, kitchen, and dining area. Blood was on the floor. The birthing chair was near the couch. He should offer to help clean up, but he didn't want Mac to notice how sluggishly he moved lately. He went over to the sink again to wash his hands a second time while he tried to decide how to help without revealing his condition.

"We don't know yet," Mac spoke up.

"Yes, we do. My baby's going to have his daddy's name," Karma cooed to the child, as if the baby had asked the question instead of Aiko.

When Gears turned around, he saw Karma flashing her husband a pointed look as her dark ponytail fell over her shoulder. As if the baby had been waiting for his name to be announced, he fell silent.

"I have a terrible name," Mac grumbled. "If you want to curse our child, you can call him Joseph."

Gears was going to break up the budding argument, but before he could speak the door to Mac's place swung open.

Chen-Ning, the youngest of the water base guards, stood in the doorway waving one arm and pulling on something outside of Gears' view. His shirt was untucked and sweat had matted his hair down. The youth's lean frame was bent over like he might fall at any moment. Blood was splattered across his shirt. Out of habit, Gears searched for an injury.

"What the hell, Chen?" Mac snapped at the interruption. "Don't you knock?"

Chen-Ning paid no attention to Karma, Dana, or Aiko. He didn't even acknowledge his boss. Instead, his entire body was actively trying to hold something on the other side of the doorway. His back flexed and bent. The lean muscles on his arms jerked.

A woman was hauled into view a second after Mac spoke. She was struggling, but Chen-Ning was holding on to her like letting go would kill him. His large hands were wrapped around both of her delicate wrists. Blood trickled through his fingers, then splashed on her shirt. A poorly made bandage was haphazardly knotted around her hand. The dark purple bandage was becoming dark brown.

Gears looked to Mac. He stared back. Neither of them knew her from the base. This was the kind of female he would remember. She was breathtaking, like an angel he'd seen drawn in a Bible. She was dressed in a flowing skirt and tight top that were different shades of purple. Her white-blonde hair was long and thick. The waves cascaded over her arm toward her ample breasts. Her appearance caused a hush as everyone stared.

Mac was the first to recover from being struck by her unnatural beauty.

"Hell. No," his friend snapped. "Not going to happen." In one swift movement, Mac picked up Gears' backpack and shoved the sack toward his chest.

"Let's talk about—" Gears didn't finish his sentence because Mac turned and used both his hands to push at Chen-Ning. Mac thrust the water base guard back out into the hallway with the woman still locked to him. Mac was in charge of the water base, and Gears knew he had wanted a few days off to spend time with his wife and new baby. His friend looked pissed that he might not get that.

"What the hell is going on, Chen? I told everyone that once my child was born, I was going to take time off. I'm not interested in bullshit." Mac didn't even wait for the door to close behind him before he started yelling. Gears trailed after them, closing the door so they wouldn't have an audience.

"Let me go." The slender woman's voice had a demanding edge. "I wish to see your healer. I must see him now."

There was something about her tone that struck a chord in Gears. He had the urge to save her. That was nonsense. He was simply an ordinary, skinny-framed medical doctor. He was also sick. He might've lied to everyone about that, but he knew the truth. He absolutely wasn't the right person to be saving a struggling, unbelievably beautiful woman. Besides, he was moving. He wasn't even going to be here to save her, even if some odd, archaic hero part of him thought it would be a good idea.

"Stop talking, witch." Chen-Ning's eyes narrowed, making them look like they were closed. The nineteen-year-old heaved her further down the hall. Her perfectly shaped lips made an angry line across her face. Even her unhappy look was exotic and lovely.

Once they were in a more open part of the walkway, Chen-Ning backed her up against the wall so Mac and Gears could fit side by side in the corridor. Since Chen-Ning was tall, he hit his arm on a wall sconce when the strange woman tugged on him a second time. The light tipped to the right, making her hair shine, and Chen-Ning released her uninjured hand. She reached for Gears, but Chen-Ning snatched her hand away before she could touch him.

"I need Gears." Chen-Ning produced a small plastic bag from his cargo pocket. Gears could see a pinky finger clearly. His eyes grew huge. Why was she missing her pinky? Who cut off her finger?

"What the fuck?" Mac snatched the bag from Chen-Ning. After looking at the finger, he handed the bag back to the guard.

"Essie asked me to watch this member of The Originals while he ran an errand, and," Chen-Ning's eyes popped to Mac's stern expression. "Then everything got shitty. I told her we were going to see Gears and she started doing a chant or something. She's a witch. You gotta help me, Doc."

The stranger stopped struggling. She stilled, and her pale blue eyes stared up at him with curiosity. Her long milky-white hair fell on one side of her face. She looked docile now, sweet and angelic.

"You're the healer here?" Her voice had a raspy quality that he liked. The sound made him think of the ocean swishing along the sand. "I pictured someone different."

Gears nodded, then reached into his bag to retrieve an instant ice pack to slow the bleeding. While he juggled the plastic sack as it got colder, his eyes dropped down her body. His intent was to look at the injury, but his eyes took the scenic route to get there.

The woman was wearing a tight purple knit top that clung to her perky breasts. The way the fabric hugged her had him thinking about taking the shirt off to see what was underneath. Removing her clothing had nothing to do with being a doctor either.

Reaching out, he placed the cold pack to her bandaged hand and tried not to look into her eyes. Instead, he stared at her skirt. It was a long garment that clung to her hips and narrow waist. The cloth brushed against his legs. On one side, above her right ankle, the clothing had been torn. The rip showed part of her smooth calf. If there was such a thing as perfect skin, she had it. Gears pictured running his hand up her leg to her inner thigh, then higher. What was wrong with him? His reaction must be due to his heart condition. He commanded his libido to calm down to ease his racing heartbeat.

"I'm shocked at your behavior." Time to stop thinking about her skin. Gears added more pressure to her wrist and frowned at the severed finger. "What were you thinking?"

Chen-Ning opened his mouth, probably to defend his actions, but Mac held up his hand.

"I don't want to hear it, Chen. Keith's supposed to be handling base issues. Not me. Damn it, I'm taking time off." Mac was looking back at the door to his room. "I'm not missing my child for The Originals shit. Not even for a hot one."

"I can't handle her, Boss. She talks weird. And now the finger!" Chen-Ning pressed her tighter to the wall, moving her away from Gears. "She's a witch, I swear it." The woman flashed a smile that produced flawless straight white teeth. Mac raised one eyebrow.

"Yes, I can see she's a real handful." Mac's voice was drenched in sarcasm. His friend looked at him. Gears shrugged. His mind had moved on to her lips. They were a lovely shade of pink.

"Tell Keith to handle her. I'm out." Mac looked back at the closed door a second time.

"Karma will be alright with the baby. She has a midwife and Doctor Dana," Gears reassured Mac. The underground base was vast. Gears had hoped that having the baby in this wing of the compound would give them some privacy. He should've known better. No one could seem to give Mac alone time with Karma.

"Karma had her baby? That's great." Chen-Ning's eyes went to the blood on Gears' lab coat. "Unless it didn't go well."

"The baby is fine." Gears pushed his glasses up his nose. "I'm surprised you didn't see him when you came barging in." Gears figured he probably sounded snide. He didn't mean to attack poor Chen-Ning. The young man was a decent guard and basically an okay guy. He just never could keep his mouth shut, and that often got him into trouble. Everyone on base thought it would be better when Brice returned and resumed the training that men like Chen-Ning needed.

"My baby's more than fine." Mac grinned broadly. Then his smile vanished as a drop of blood dripped onto his boot. "But are we going to deal with this woman bleeding? I think you all talk too much."

Gears stepped closer to Chen-Ning's captive again and held the ice pack to her hand while putting pressure on her wrist. Mac was right, he needed to help her. He shouldn't be standing here in the hall envying his best friend. Problem was, whenever Gears thought about the new baby in the other room, jealousy reared its head. There was a good chance he would never have kids. There were so few females to meet in the Northern Earth Dens. So many died of Snow Flu, and the rest wanted strong, healthy males. The handful of women he did meet wanted the security his position offered, not him as a man. That type of relationship was complicated, and so far, he hadn't thought it deserved his time to figure out.

"Best wishes." Chen-Ning shrugged.

The end of the congratulations came out in a puff of air as the woman wiggled her good hand out of his grasp and tried to get closer to Gears' side. Chen-Ning snatched her free arm back.

"Who is this?" Gears asked because he could tell his best friend was distracted. Mac was looking back at his room again. If Gears thought about it, he was still shocked that he'd delivered a child. He hoped that one day there would be more children. Maybe he could deliver a baby again if the underground population grew. First, he'd cure Snow Flu, then he could do the doctor thing again. That was if he could figure out a way to manage his heart condition. A part of him wasn't accepting the idea that he might die. He still had dreams.

"This is Hunter's girlfriend, Luna." Chen-Ning tugged her flat against the wall. The guard was five inches taller than her. Even though they looked like they might weigh the same, Chen-Ning's height gave him a slight advantage. "She's part of a deal with The Originals. Keith told me to keep her in interrogation until they were ready for the trade."

"Then *you* should be there with her." Mac's voice was steel. "Karma and I are spending time with the baby. Not the baby and a crazy Original. I'm out."

Chen-Ning turned to Gears. "Can you at least close the hole from her missing finger before I put her back in interrogation?" The young man's eyes widened hopefully.

"I have to pack. I'm leaving in a few days. I'm working on the information the C.T.O.N.A. released about Snow Flu." Gears gave his practiced response for when people asked what he was doing.

"But you're not leaving for a few days." Chen-Ning squinted. "You can help me now."

Luna stopped moving.

"Are you going to H.S.P.C. Headquarters in Dallas? I'd like that very much." Her eyes captured Gears' attention. Luna's eyes were like sparkling pools of clear blue water. He felt like he was falling forward, swimming… drowning.

"I'm going—"

Mac cut him off. "Gears, fix the finger. Don't engage with a member of The Originals. Even if she's hot." Mac started back down the hall.

"She's not hot." Gears denied the obvious. He was being contradictory in the hope that Mac wouldn't be able to see how attractive he thought Luna was.

"I swear, Gears, you might be a robot." Mac put his hand on the knob. "After she's pieced back together, Chen, return her to where you were supposed to be and wait for directions from Keith. I've got a baby to see."

"Listen to Aiko and Dana," Gears threw at his friend before Mac let the door slam. Gears guessed that was his final say on the matter.

"Come on, old man." Chen-Ning turned to head toward Gears' room, tugging the woman with him. While she twisted against the guard, she kept her enchanting eyes on Gears. Her intense gaze was a little disconcerting. Gears trudged after the two of them.

"Why can't you leave Luna with Keith?" Gears asked as he gestured for Chen-Ning to hold the cold ice pack to Luna's hand while they walked.

"The Originals captured Brice. Keith is negotiating a trade with their leader. His name is Hunter. I hear Hunter is a real asshole. If we get Brice back, then Hunter can have his girlfriend back. I'm going to send him the finger. It's a shame it's not her middle one. That'd be funny, like a big up yours, douche bag."

"You're not going to send her finger anywhere." Gears was horrified at the idea. "I'm going to reattach it."

"You can have it," Luna cut in. "Send my finger to Hunter. I just wanted to see your healer. Besides, Rumi says 'The wound is the place the light enters you.'"

"She's a witch. Crazy witch," Chen-Ning muttered. He held up the appendage. "Witches might be hot to confuse us. She needs a wart on her nose."

"You shouldn't have cut her finger off to begin with," Gears admonished the young man. "Witch or not."

"I didn't," Chen-Ning sputtered. "She got my knife off my belt and cut off her own finger. She was doing magic on me. I don't get distracted. I'm a good guard."

Gears pushed up his glasses as his eyebrows rose. He refrained from waving the bullshit flag on that comment.

"Really, I'm a good guard," Chen-Ning repeated.

"She wasn't doing magic." Gears couldn't come up with why she would have severed her own finger. Maybe to be free? Did she think that Hunter wouldn't believe she was here otherwise? Women were on his list of enigmas he might never fully understand.

Together, the three of them reached his room.

While Chen-Ning pulled a length of rope from his other cargo pocket and tied her wrist, Gears unlocked his door. Chen-Ning brushed past him and hauled Luna over to Gears' bed.

"Is that really necessary?" Gears pointed to the rope.

"Yes." Chen added another knot. "I'm going to tie her to the bed so you can work on her."

Gears decided not to argue. On the wall to his right was a dresser with six large drawers. Each one was labeled, and his label maker sat on the top. Gears crouched down in front of the one marked "cords."

"I got one." Gears dug around until he found a long, thick, durable rope. Behind him, he could hear Chen-Ning muttering to the knots. Due to Chen-Ning's perpetually running mouth, he was a loner. Since he'd been accepted as a water base guard, he'd managed to alienate or anger just about everyone who'd come in contact with him. Gears had the feeling that Chen-Ning was used to talking to himself. Heaven knew no one on this base had the patience to listen to him.

Gears spun around holding the rope. Chen-Ning sat Luna on the center of his bed. He lifted the woman's hands over her head. She was willowy, and her wrists looked like they might break in the guard's grip. The ripped fabric that was acting like a bandage over her severed finger was still tightly wound around her hand.

"Hurry up, Doc, or I might get blood on your blanket."

"I'll stay here with the healer. You may leave now. No need to tie me to the bed." Luna stared at Chen-Ning.

"Don't listen to her. She'll turn your brain to mushed bananas." Chen secured the rope. "Hand me the other rope."

Gears did as he was told. He stayed as far away from Luna as he could while Chen-Ning gripped the ends of the ties. Efficiency wasn't Chen-Ning's strong suit. After a few minutes of struggling and mumbling, the water base guard finally had her hands tied to the pipes that made up the head of Gears' queen-sized bed. The guard stepped back as if to survey his handiwork. Studying Chen-Ning made Gears feel older than his late twenties. Watching Chen-Ning was like looking at a monkey putting on lipstick. It was funny and all, but also highly ridiculous.

Gears turned away and started gathering medical supplies from the counter on the far side of the room. Chen-Ning started to pace.

When Gears returned to the bedside, he almost ran into the guard, who was walking a trench into the tiles. Gears frowned. He wasn't going to be able to focus with Chen-Ning breathing down his neck the whole time.

"Chen? Don't you have something you could be doing?"

"Like?"

"Like not bothering me?"

Chen-Ning walked back and forth by the bed a few more times, then frowned. "I guess while you work on her, I could go and check in with Essie. Maybe Keith is back, or he sent a message. That is, if you think you can handle her."

"I can handle this. Go." Gears wasn't sure if he was telling the truth. Luna looked first to her bound hands, then to his eyes. Her eyes were intense and curious. Gears thought the large blue orbs sparkled like effervescing liquid. The idea that eyes could glitter had never entered his head before. Taking a shaky breath, he noted that his heart was beating too hard again. That was odd. He wasn't doing anything taxing. He was simply standing there before a woman.

"Are you going to help me, healer?" Luna whispered to him. His stomach fluttered.

"Healer? Just call me Gears." Gears thought his voice sounded funny. He hoped Chen-Ning didn't notice. He cleared his throat. "I'm a doctor. I'm going to look at your hand." He was having trouble breathing. It was his heart, not her.

"There you go, old man." Chen-Ning handed him the pinky finger in the bag, then walked to the exit. "You might have to do some fancy explaining if your girlfriend shows up." Chen-Ning scratched at his short black hair. "Sorry about that."

"You have a girlfriend?" Luna sat up straighter and frowned. "I have feelings about this."

What an awkward subject. Gears shot a glare at Chen-Ning.

"I'm single," he muttered.

"Got a one-way ticket to Dumpsville? Been there." Chen-Ning chuckled. With every moment that passed, Gears was getting a firmer idea why he wasn't well liked.

"We mutually communicated our requirements for the relationship and then consented to go our separate ways," Gears explained.

"Sounds swanky." Chen-Ning shrugged. "Better than 'I got anally raped with no lube.'"

Gears shook his head at Chen-Ning. He didn't even know how to respond to that.

"She didn't love you," Luna piped up. "She wasn't your perfect match. Mother calls it your Conpar. Would you like to share with me?"

His eyes popped to Luna's earnest expression. She was right, but he didn't say that out loud. His ex-girlfriend hadn't loved him. It was more that she'd liked the idea of him. She had loved living on a nice comfortable water base with a doctor around to care for her elderly parents. He had figured out that she wanted him only as a means to an end. Since he was heading to H.S.P.C. HQ in Dallas, he'd upset her tidy schedule. She didn't want to leave her family, and he had no choice because of his heart.

"It isn't necessary to cover my past relationship history to mend your hand." He hoped both Luna and Chen-Ning would leave the topic.

Luna tilted her head to the side. He got the notion she wasn't going to abandon the subject.

"The breakup doesn't bother you, does it? Do you want to share how you're feeling? All emotions have a place within us. It's okay to feel."

"I don't need a therapist," he snapped. Who did this woman think she was? Yes, she was right. It did bother him that the breakup didn't trouble him at all. He should've cared or mourned or something, but it was none of her business. They were strangers. Didn't she understand that?

Gears slapped down a medical bandage on the stool next to his bed. Why was he annoyed? He didn't generally react in anger to anyone. She was just some lost stranger. He would help her then move on.

"Let's drop this." Gears gave her a reassuring smile then nodded to Chen-Ning. He was more concerned that if he told people about the breakup they would start asking questions. That's all this was. If people, meaning Mac, asked about where his girlfriend had gone, it might come out that he was sick. His illness had been the only factor that he cared about during the split.

Gears got a fresh pack of ice from his freezer. He stood next to Luna's hand.

"I'm going to untie her." Gears fingered the ropes. Luna was so fragile. He felt like he should take better care of her.

"No, Doc!" Chen-Ning's slanted eyes flashed wide. "Don't untie her no matter what she says. Don't listen to her. Don't talk to her and don't let her touch anything. Whatever she says is mystical voodoo. She's a witch."

Chen-Ning was serious. Gears barely kept from laughing out loud. He was a man of logic. There was no mystical voodoo. If he was worried about anything right now, it was the way his temperature seemed to edge a few degrees higher when he looked at her. Half of the time he wasn't sure if he was irritated by her or turned on. Both were not acceptable responses. He would take care of her hand, then never see her again. No voodoo required.

"You gave me a long list of what not to do. What do you want me *to* do?"

"Fix her hand, then go about whatever you normally do. I'll be right back. Pretend like she isn't even here."

Pretend she wasn't here? Impossible.

Still, he had packing to do. He also needed to get cleaned up after the birth of the baby. If she stopped talking and he got into his work, then having her here would be fine with him.

"So, go already." Gears nodded to the guard.

"Don't untie her," Chen-Ning said.

Gears wasn't a child. He understood that you didn't mess with The Originals, even gorgeous ones. However, she didn't seem so dangerous.

"I'm just going to fix her hand."

"I'll be right back." The young man left the room with another curt nod and one last glance at the stranger.

After he was gone, Gears stripped off his bloody lab coat while trying to decide what he was going to do next. Her bleeding had slowed considerably, but if he upset the wound it wasn't going to be pleasant. Did he have any drugs on hand to help her deal with the pain? He took a mental inventory of what was in his backpack and in the cabinets in his room.

"This is going to hurt. I'm going to give you drugs." He rummaged in his backpack. "I think I have something you can take orally. Or I have a shot, which'll work faster. Do you want pills or a shot?"

"Mother didn't tell me that you'd be handsome. I can see that your soul is quite stunning. It calls to me." Luna twisted against the ropes so she could look up at him.

Gears' head popped out of his bag. His hope that she might stop talking vanished. The idea that she could be mentally unstable crossed his mind. It would be a shame if such a lovely woman were completely unbalanced.

"Is that a yes or a no to the drugs?" Gears was a doctor, sometimes a chemist, and he dabbled in biomedical engineering when he got bored. He wasn't a psychotherapist. Figuring out if she was nuts wasn't in his job description. He concentrated on her wound.

"You're very kind." Luna was focusing her femininity on him like a spotlight. "Kind and pleasant to look at. We'll be happy together." She paused. "For however long we get."

"What?" Gears felt a sensation of falling forward into her eyes.

"I told Mother I didn't really get attracted to men. But Rumi says 'Lovers don't finally meet somewhere. They're in each other all along.'"

"Your mother?" What was she talking about? Gears shook his head. He needed to keep his wits about him and his eyes above her chin. Focusing on her injury was best. He ruthlessly crushed all other emotions down.

"There's a young girl that I met when I was ten years old. Her nickname is Mother. She told me about you. I've been waiting to meet you for a long time."

Gears struggled in vain to block out her words. Instead, he loosened the bandage and kept himself from staring. Concentrating on her hand was essential. He was happy her wrists were above her head. Less blood loss. His fingers began to release the knot at the top of the dressing.

"Healer?"

Gears tried not to, but he couldn't help looking at Luna again. *Don't ask.* Her sultry gaze had him mesmerized in moments.

"What?"

"I don't need your help to mend my skin. I can do it on my own."

So, she *was* crazy. Gears didn't need a medical degree for that diagnosis.

"What?"

"I can do it by myself, but I'd like you to watch. May you join me?"

"What?" Gears had no clue what she was talking about. And "may you join me" didn't sound right.

His eyes went to the exit. Chen-Ning wasn't going to save him. Maybe the guard had had a point earlier. Why was he so captivated by her? He wasn't in the mood to figure out that riddle. Gears disliked things that were random, unpredictable, or unexpected. Luna was all three.

"Take off the bandage. I'll heal myself, we'll talk." Even though Luna's sentence was preposterous, her soft voice was hypnotic. "And then, together, you and I will do other things to heal…"

Gears' hands paused as he considered what she asked of him. He felt the urge to heal her no matter what her request, but he should honor her wishes, shouldn't he? He wasn't a fan of illogical actions. His eyes dropped to the rope. There was no reason to do what she wanted, but it was her body to do with as she saw fit. Good heavens. Why was he so unsure of himself around her?

He did as she asked even though freeing her was going to cause more bleeding.

The bloody cloth dropped to the blue rug next to his bed. Gears waited for a gush from her missing finger. It didn't come. He blinked over and over. He was hallucinating. The injury was an open hole. Before his eyes, the skin pulled together by itself. Gears gawked like a simpleton. After the skin had met tightly over the hole, the area looked like the tissue was being melted together. The way it sealed reminded him of candle wax.

After maybe a minute, there was not even a scar. The skin on Luna's hand was smooth. No finger, but flat, smooth skin over her hand as if she had never had a finger to begin with.

Gears' brain refused to believe what he saw. He needed to figure out what had happened. How had she accomplished this?

"What…?" He couldn't come up with a logical explanation. "Did you just…?" Gears couldn't put together a sentence. That was unlike him. Why weren't his gears turning? He reached out and brushed his fingers over where the hole had been. Smooth, soft skin greeted him.

"You do not believe what you see?" Luna's voice was coaxing. "We cannot see God, but we can believe. The universe is a mysterious place. People are complex and multifaceted. I believed in you long before we met today."

"There has to be a rational explanation." His brain began to flip through all possible ways she could have accomplished this. First off, maybe this was all a joke. She never had a finger. What if this was a prank Chen-Ning was playing on him? His eyes dropped to the bloody bandage on the floor. Next, his eyes jumped to her torn skirt. How did they play this trick on him?

"I have come here to see you, Healer. I want to mend your broken heart." Luna was still staring at him. He wanted her to stop watching him so his brain would work the way it was supposed to. Chen-Ning had been correct. His brain *was* turning to mushed bananas. He took a hasty step away from the bed. A wave of dizziness hit him.

"I don't believe in magic. Did Keith or Chen-Ning tell you this would be funny?"

"I'm asking for you to untie me, so we can begin." Luna frowned. "I've been waiting for you for a long time."

Second option, Gears was going insane. People didn't heal themselves. His mind spun. Why weren't his gears turning? His mind always worked. Always. Why couldn't he solve this conundrum? His heart was pounding again.

"Wait, fix my what?" One beat, two beats.

"Your heart." Luna wiggled on the bed, then leaned her head against the pipe headboard. "I'll explain. May you sit here with me and listen with an open mind? No judgments. I need you to connect to your heart-mind. It is a place of peace and understanding."

Sitting down sounded like a superb idea. Gears glanced at the bed. Better not sit next to her. Gears turned around and grabbed a stool he'd been using as a bedside table. He picked up the items resting on the top and set them on the floor.

"I need a book on proper English." He pulled the stool near the bed and sank down. "I don't think 'May you sit here with me' is correct. I'd like to look it up."

"Rumi says, 'The quieter you become, the more you are able to hear.'"

Chapter 3

"This is how I would die into the love I have for

you: as pieces of cloud dissolve in sunlight."

Rumi~

Quiet wasn't his favorite thing, especially when he had about ten different unanswered questions floating in his head. He didn't want silence, he wanted her to tell him what was going on.

"Did you cut off your finger?" Gears asked. "Like Chen-Ning said?"

"Yes. I cut off my finger for one simple reason." Luna nodded. "I wanted to meet you. I also considered that it would be a way to show you my power. It is our destiny to meet. You're my Conpar."

"You cut off a finger to meet me?" Gears adjusted his glasses. "A note or letter of invitation would've probably worked just as well."

"Have you ever met anyone with a talent that you couldn't explain? I'm told the H.S.P.C. has others who are special."

"Gifted."

"Alright, gifted," Luna agreed.

Mac knew when someone was lying. Karma could see in the dark. He had tested them both. And then there was Essie. After meeting Essie, Luna shouldn't have surprised him, yet she did.

His brain started to go over all the ways Luna might be able to heal her skin. Of all the many ideas he considered, none of them involved voodoo or Luna being a witch. He had a few theories on an evolutionary jump. Perhaps the Earth was trying to give mankind a little something extra to survive after the ice took over. If he had more time to live he could research a hypothesis.

Living. He wanted to do that. His mind returned to Luna's sentence. She wanted to heal his heart. Could she do that? How did she know he had heart problems?

"I know of people who have gifts, or talents if you want to call them that." He would start by exploring that possibility first.

"I knew you would be a man whose brain is his servant, not his master." Luna smiled at him. "And now I'll heal you as I'm meant to do. The universe has a plan for us. Even if I'm Juliet and you're Romeo."

There were a handful of things in that last sentence that Gears wanted to discuss with her, but he figured he should stick to the most important topic. Fixing his heart.

"How did you know my heart is…" Gears paused. "Broken." Best to use her words, so there would be less confusion. Gears felt like he needed a manual to understand most of what Luna said.

"Mother told me that I would be your downfall. She told me you would die when your heart stopped beating.

She can see the future. I plan to change that. I won't be your downfall. I'm going to heal you."

So, that equally answered and didn't answer his question. He was left with more doubts rolling around in his head. Okay. Maybe if he simply found out about the how, not the why. He would try a new angle.

"You said you could heal my broken heart. How do you want to do that?"

"I also knew you would be the kind of man who likes to get to the point. I appreciate that. I also like clarity."

Maybe she *liked* clarity, but Gears didn't think she was good at it.

"How do you expect to…" Gears trailed off. What words could he use to get her to understand his question? More important than that, what did he say to get her to properly answer him when he asked a second time?

"Expectations in life are like fragile glass. The tighter you hold on to them, the more they crack."

"Maybe you should start at the beginning?" Gears ground his teeth together. His patience dangled by a thread. Rarely in his life had he ever felt like shaking someone, but Luna was testing his imperturbability.

"Yes. The beginning. First, I made sure to escape Hunter and then be captured by the H.S.P.C. to come here to see you. It's my right as your Conpar, your match. Then I cut off my finger. We met. Rumi says—"

"Stop quoting a thirteenth-century poet for a second." About six questions popped up in his brain after she spoke, but the first issue plagued him the most. Why was she using the term Conpar? He was reasonably certain it was from a different language.

"Try this. Why do you want to help me? Why do you think we're a…" Gears reviewed his rusty Latin. "Conpar? We've never met, and I'm H.S.P.C., and you are part of The Originals. We aren't matched to do anything."

Luna laughed. It was a throaty sound, incredibly sexy. The noise made his cock twitch awake. He shifted on the stool. The sexual attraction was a curious sensation. Maybe he felt something because she was so beautiful, but that was completely out of character. He'd never judged a person by their looks before and there was no reason to start now. Besides, even if he did think her amazing, he was average. What could Luna possibly see in him? Romantic relationships weren't even on his radar to solve. He would cure his heart, then Snow Flu, then maybe a few other things. When he was old and gray, only then would he try to figure out women.

"I'm Original, and you are H.S.P.C. So I'm Juliet, and you're Romeo. Just because the houses feud, that doesn't stop love."

Gears cocked one eyebrow at her, then pushed up his glasses. Luna just went from Rumi to Shakespeare and tossed in a Latin word for fun. She talked in circles, and he was getting sucked into it. He was nonplussed at the sudden change in subject.

"*Romeo and Juliet* is the story of a couple of teenagers who both died."

"We won't." Luna's eyes flipped to her hands. "May you untie me now?"

"I shouldn't." Gears frowned. Untying Luna would be foolish and irrational. He didn't even need to loosen the rope now that she was fine. Also, she hadn't answered any of his questions.

"I mean," Luna smiled, "Will you untie me now? I can heal you."

Healed. Maybe Luna could heal him. Everything he had done up to this point hadn't worked. Was God giving him a chance to live? It would be a great leap of faith to let her go. He pictured her hand. She definitely had a gift. As unsound as this was, he was desperate. Good heavens, he was going to free her.

"I must be losing all my marbles." Rising from the stool, he began to release the ropes. If she tried to run away, he would stand over her ready. One knot slipped open, then the second. The cords fell. For a single heartbeat, she didn't move.

"You don't need marbles, you need me." Luna's eyes caught his as she lowered her hands to her lap. "I'd like to wash the blood away before we begin."

Lord, what next? Tarot cards? Astrology? Was the moon in the right house for his heart to beat?

Gears decided not to ask. He had the feeling this woman would reply with a bunch of Rumi quotes mixed with Shakespeare that would have him questioning his IQ. Never before had he felt stupid. Right now, that was exactly how he felt. He took one step away from the bed and she rose gracefully. Eye to eye, they faced each other.

"Over there," he muttered. His right hand gestured with an awkward wave to the sink. Luna nodded and stepped past him. She didn't make a run for the door. His muscles relaxed.

"Where's the soap, my match?" Luna stood next to the sink with the water running over her hands.

Gears pointed to a bar next to the sink. This "match" term was bothering him. He wasn't hers, and she wasn't his. They didn't match up, this wasn't a dating service.

"You do understand that we've never met before, right?" It occurred to him that she could have a serious brain issue. "Did you hit your head at all?" He went over the symptoms of concussions.

"Our souls were united long before we were born. Mother speaks Latin, and she calls it Conpar, which translates to perfect match or a mate." Luna hooked her fingers under her shirt and easily lifted the garment over her head. "She thinks we should all find our match." She threw the purple top to the floor between them.

Gears' brain emptied as his jaw went slack.

"What?" He wasn't sure if he was asking about why she had just taken off her shirt or why they were discussing Latin words. He pushed his glasses up his nose. This was starting to feel surreal. Luna was out of his league in both beauty and her confusing mind. They didn't belong together. He was going to be direct, firm, and sensible when he explained that to her.

"You say 'what' a lot." Luna washed her arms, then face. Water splashed on her creamy white skin. She reminded him of a porcelain doll. Drops of water clung to her pink lips. They trickled downward, leading his eyes to her powder blue bra. She stood after she drank from the faucet and shut off the water. More water made a path down her neck. The glistening droplets vanishing between her breasts might've been the hottest thing he'd ever seen. He'd never thought of water as sexual, but he was completely confident Luna had forever changed his view.

"I don't say 'what' a lot," he mumbled. Blood rushed to his groin. It was time to get his head together. The head he used for thinking.

Gears bent down to pick up her blouse, hoping she would put it back on. He held the garment out.

She ignored him.

He felt like a shard of iron coming too close to an extremely powerful magnet. One step closer and he would be drawn in.

Take the shirt, he thought over and over again. She gripped both sides of her long skirt and yanked down. Heavens, that was not what he wanted her to do. The fabric fluttered then landed in a pile at her ankles. Standing before him, Luna looked like a Nordic goddess, pagan and untamed.

Gears thought for the second time that this must be a hoax. Looking back at the door, he presumed someone would burst in and yell, "Got ya!"

No door opened.

Gears glanced back at the exquisiteness of Luna while he still held her shirt. Her lightweight blue cotton bra complimented her eyes. Her underwear was the same shade of white-blonde as her hair. His eyes were glued to her legs and the fabric. Maybe it wasn't that the fabric was light colored. On second thought, Gears had the idea that the underwear was sheer. Lace cuddled her thighs. What precious equilibrium he retained spun into infinity.

How long had he been gaping? He brought his eyes up to her face. She angled her head to the side like she was confused. No way did she get to be the one who was perplexed. He was the one who didn't know what was going on. He was still holding out her top. He waved it back and forth, hoping she would take it.

"Luna…" he began, but she stepped out of her skirt and he forgot words existed. Once free of the dress, she kicked off one shoe, then the other. The sneakers bounced and landed near the bed.

"Make love to me." The sentence was tossed at him like a bauble. She then reached for the garment he was still clutching. After she had taken the item from his hand, she dropped it to the floor. "Don't hold back."

"What?" Good God, maybe he did say that a lot. He bent down to pick up her shirt again. He was shocked and flattered that she apparently wanted to have sex with him. He pushed up his glasses. Actually, he was more shocked that he was flattered at her proposition.

It was time to get his brain to turn on. Time to think. What should he do first? Get her dressed, or at least covered, so he would stop panting.

He held her top out again. Luna crossed the small space between them. She took her shirt and once more tossed it to the floor.

"It's time."

"What?" Gears pushed up his glasses. "I mean, time for what?"

"Unleash your desire, my match. Let go of your emotions to free the power inside of you." Luna kissed his cheek gently. "Connect with me and I will heal your heart." Her hand lifted to his chest. "Can you feel it?"

Luna stared at him with hungry eyes. Gears had the feeling this was a now-or-never moment, as if she was giving herself over to him for safekeeping. An unexplainable yet tremendous force inside of him demanded he accept her offer. Yes, he could feel it. The craving, the compulsion, the yearning was the most unscientific experience that had ever happened to him. This was a dangerous situation, like mixing hydrogen and oxygen then waiting for a spark.

He took a hasty step back.

Something silvery flickered in her eyes, as fast as a moving fish in a pool of water. Luna's fingers went to a clasp at the front of her bra. The fabric shifted, then dropped. Gears tried to hold in the lust, but for the first time in his life, he tried to do something and failed miserably. Lord above, he wanted her. He couldn't stop himself. It was wrong, but his body didn't care. She stood stationary. Her breasts were fully exposed to him, and her tiny sheer silk panties barely covered her mound. He took a hesitant step forward, trying to force his mind to control the terrible heat that was spreading in his body.

Keeping himself together wasn't working. His palms began to sweat. Luna reached out and unfastened the top button on his jeans. His cock needed zero encouragement. His crazy penis had been prepared for her since he'd met her. Luna bent her head, and her cloud-like hair fell in waves over her shoulder. The locks slid over her breasts as he reached for her. Pulling her into his arms, he felt like someone else was taking over.

Luna didn't pull away from him. A part of him wanted her to, and another part insisted that she stay within his grasp. Gears drew her tightly to his sweater and wished he was naked. Her soft curves against his frame felt so incredible, so right. His penis ached for liberation. A whisper of thought nagged at him. The only place he was going to find relief and healing might be in her silken depth.

Since they were the same height, Gears put his right hand on the back of her neck to bring her face closer. He stared into her blue eyes as he slid his left hand to her breast to fondle one of her nipples. He squeezed the stiff peak between his fingers softly, then put his lips near her ear. She shivered.

"I'm not normally like this. I like to think about what I'm doing." His voice dropped lower as he whispered to her. Senses awakened that pumped languorously through his blood like syrup.

"Feel me, Gears. Don't be in your head. Be here." Luna placed her palm over his heart. He felt like the organ was beating into her hand. "Submit to love without thinking."

Something wild and forbidden that he never let out of himself was ripping free. This was getting a little out of control. Who was he kidding? This was out of control like Mt. Vesuvius.

Gears leaned forward and his mouth claimed hers. His tongue found its way inside and everything in her rose to greet him. Her kiss had all the power and intensity of a nuclear explosion. Within seconds they were touching, petting, tugging on one another, as though they had been waiting for this moment their entire lives. Luna sucked his lower lip and moaned when he grabbed her bottom to squeeze tight. Every nerve ending was tuned into this woman.

He rolled her nipple between his fingers again, then stooped down to meet the light pink areola. He hadn't had a lot of sex in his life, but he was knowledgeable about women's bodies. Her nipple came into focus, and he slid his tongue out and over the tip. He eased away slowly and blew while he hooked his hands under the edge of his sweater. A smile kicked up one side of his face as her nipple reacted to the cool air.

As he grabbed his sweater and undershirt, it struck him that he was removing them like they were on fire. He ripped the garments off savagely. He wasn't a teenager, but that was how Luna made him feel. Once his shirts hit the floor, he returned to teasing her. Quickly he began to lick all the supple skin of her breasts. He nuzzled the soft undersides as he argued with himself about whether this was a bad idea or not. She moaned as her hands rose to his hair, yanking his head tighter to her chest. Gears drew her nipple into his mouth as a growl came from a secretive place deep inside of him. This wasn't him, but he couldn't stop. Maybe she really was a witch. Sucking lightly, he worked her other breast with his hand as he edged down her body. He tugged on her nipple, and the tight point hardened for him even more. Perfect, just like all of her.

"Luna, you're beautiful," he whispered to her skin. Long-denied urges uncoiled in his chest. Something primitive and uncontrollable threatened to erupt. He held on to his self-control by the flimsiest of fibers.

"Rumi says 'The beauty you see in me is a reflection of you.'" Luna used both hands to slip his glasses off his face. She let them drop to the growing pile of clothes on the floor. He felt naked under her gaze. "You're handsome, but your soul is beautiful." Her eyes were so full of lust that it went straight to his knees. His legs buckled and he dropped to the tiles before her.

"Gears?" His name sounded intimate on her lips, almost an endearment.

He didn't answer. Tugging at Luna's panties, he slipped them down her thighs. The tuft of neatly trimmed blonde curls hidden beneath smelled of a unique aroma that was all Luna. Gears inhaled deeply through his nose. His eyes flicked shut for a moment. Licking her hip, he continued to work her panties off. Once the fabric was free of her ankles, he tossed them aside.

Eyeing maybe the most exquisite female anatomy he had ever seen, he feathered his fingers up her legs.

Parting her folds, he began to lick along the outer edge of her sex. Luna jerked slightly, and he used his other hand to keep her steady. Some part of his brain thought he should stop or ask her if this was okay, but the animal part of him overruled the notion. He wanted her. There was nothing more than that.

Kneading her ass cheek, Gears let his tongue glide delicately over the rim of her clit.

"Gears," Luna panted as she clutched at his hair. She swayed her hips, easing herself onto his face.

"Please don't ask me to stop," he murmured into her slit.

"I won't."

He smiled at her as juice dripped along the inside of her thighs. Lapping it up like a dog, he growled. Again. She tasted fantastic. Luna was like sweet, ripe fruit. She fed a growing fire in him he hadn't expected. It was a raw, visceral need.

Luna rocked her hips into his lips and mouth. She pressed herself against his face with no shame or shyness. Varying the degree at which he sucked on her bud, Gears felt Luna's legs begin to shake. She quivered as her orgasm flooded her. Her climax came on suddenly, and he eagerly savored the cream that trickled from her body.

"Gears, please." Luna pulled on his short hair a second time.

Reluctantly, like he was leaving an old friend, he gave in and pulled his head away from the junction of her thighs. He stood, and was surprised that he was slightly dizzy. What was he doing?

"Stop?" He prayed she would say stop. He couldn't leave her, so she was going to have to be the one to end this. Hormones, his rioting testosterone, it was all somehow affecting his judgment.

"No."

The lure of her mouth was too great. Thoughts vanished again. Gears clamped his mouth over hers and started to seek her tongue and her permission to keep on.

She bit at him playfully, then skillfully received his tongue just when he thought he should cease this madness.

Luna encircled him with her hands. He wanted to throw her on his bed and mount her. He didn't do things like that, but that was what he wanted to do this second. She broke their kiss and dropped to her knees before he could do anything. Reaching down, he ran his hands over her jaw as she nipped at his fingers

"It's my turn to taste you."

"What?"

She giggled and worked her hands into the front of his jeans, then began to slide them down his hips. When his cock bobbed out before her hand, she laughed again.

"The healer doesn't wear underwear?"

"Luna, that's right, I'm a healer, a doctor. I have principles."

"Principles?" she repeated.

"Integrity."

"Integrity?" Luna reminded him of a parrot he'd once had. A parrot with a sexy voice.

"I didn't expect to…" To what? To feel like this with her? To feel like this with anyone, ever?

"Expectations in life are like—"

"Right. I remember."

She met his gaze and smiled. Her blue eyes were lit up like his cock was a Christmas present. How was he going to say no to her? That's right. He wasn't going to say no. Integrity was just going to have to take a hit today.

"I'm starving for you," she whispered. Gears felt powerful knowing he was going to be the one who would satisfy her. He forgot the code of conduct he lived by. He forgot everything but her eyes.

She moved his pants down a bit more, and he felt like he was caught in a trap. Wrapping her hand around his long shaft, delight lit her features. Gears moaned, and she mirrored the noise as she ran her hand up and down the full length of his erection. She let her tongue flick out and over the head before taking him fully into her mouth.

His body jolted as if touching a live wire with wet hands.

"Good heavens." Gears closed his eyes in ecstasy as Luna took him all the way in. When he felt her gag reflex kick in, Gears almost shot his seed down her throat.

"We… just…" He didn't even know what he was saying anymore.

Luna continued to move over his shaft. Each time he hit the back of her throat, they moaned together. This woman was better than any woman he could ever imagine. Watching Luna on her knees before him, with her mouth sucking him, he felt like a different person. He was no longer a skinny, sick medical doctor. He was… a king, a warrior, a hero. No one had ever made him feel like this.

Gears wound his fingers through her snowy hair while her blue eyes stared up at him. She worked him to the brink of orgasm, then just as he thought he might explode, she halted.

"I need you to be inside of me for the energy to connect fully. I'm asking you to enter me. May you do that for me?"

Gears was panting so hard that for a moment he couldn't speak, let alone think. At this time, he was pretty sure she could ask him for anything, and he would give it to her. Their mutual desire was a third person in the room.

"Yes." Linking his hand in hers, Gears tugged her over to his bed. He kicked off his shoes and stepped out of his jeans as he went. Luna climbed up and arranged herself over the covers. He couldn't help but think she was even more magnificent spread before him like this. Her long hair was fanned out around her head, and her pale blue eyes gazed at him intently. His chest began to grow tight. She was so willing for him, a virtual stranger, to let him do whatever he wanted. This couldn't be right.

"Gears," she whispered. The one word baptized his soul.

Everything about her called to him. The taste of her clit was still fresh in his mind and on his lips. Unable to control himself, he leaned over to sample the sweetness of her again. Parting her velvety folds, he inserted a finger into her hot channel. He brought his lips to her swollen bundle of nerves and sucked the hard nub into his mouth. The taste of her was divine.

Luna gasped then bucked beneath him as he varied the suction on her clit. Her fingers dug into his sheets. She was so hot, so tight. She was so… his.

As she wiggled under the weight of his mouth and hands, he felt her climax rising again. Yes. He wanted her to reach that peak. He didn't slow his onslaught. Lavishing a series of long licks over her slit, he rode her explosion with her. He drank from her. She wiggled more, and her sweet honey flowed. Cream coated his fingers, and he wetted his lips with her unique scent.

Luna tugged at the sides of his face. When his eyes met hers, he saw blatant need shining at him.

"Adam, please."

He didn't even try to figure out how she knew his real name. The knowledge that she desired him as much as he desired her sent his emotions soaring high. Sliding up over her, he settled himself between her legs. He came to rest right above her in a semi-pushup. The head of his penis was positioned at her cleft. He was so close to heaven.

She rotated slightly under him, causing the head of his erection to enter her tight core. His arms tightened as he strained to keep from ramming into her like a madman.

He took a few calming breaths, wanting this to last forever. He wasn't the type of man to take her roughly, but he would satisfy her. She was his addiction right now. Though it was wrong to have sex with a stranger, a captive, he couldn't seem to care.

"Now." There was a soft begging note to Luna's words that ripped into his heart and wouldn't let go. "Slide deeper inside of me."

Unable to resist her wet slit any longer, Gears did as she asked. He thrust himself deep into her until he was all the way to his balls.

Pulling out to the tip, he locked gazes with her. She smiled, then closed her eyes.

"No." He gripped her chin. "I want you to look at me, Luna. I want you to know that you're with me. This might be wrong, but I want you to know that it's me who's going to make you orgasm."

A slow grin spread across her face. She ran her hand the length of their intertwined bodies. Gears' cock jerked when she wrapped her fingers around him, and he fought to control himself.

"I'm with you, Conpar." She let go of him. "This isn't wrong. This is perfect."

Gears slammed into her, making her cry out and grab his arms. He pumped rapidly, causing the bed to wobble. Heat and energy infused him mixed with a raw, undiluted emotion that he couldn't identify. Stopping was out of the question even if someone might be able to hear the way the bed was hitting the wall.

Luna's channel gripped him. He tried to slow down to delay his ejaculation. He switched to making a swirling pattern with his hips, but it didn't keep his orgasm at bay.

Luna clawed his back.

"Yes, Gears. More."

But he couldn't give her more. He was going to come, and she wasn't there yet. He didn't have the stamina for the intense squeezing of his shaft. Vibrant currents ran between the two of them. His body tingled. He was too close. He tried frantically to calm the inner fire.

Luna's pink lips were swollen from his kisses and her cheeks were rosy. She was teetering on the edge. He could feel her climax in his body, almost as if it were his own. Her orgasm called to his. She wrapped her legs around his hips, and the action forced him to penetrate her deeply. Sliding all the way to her very center caused his entire being to celebrate.

She undid him in that one move. Everything inside of him unraveled. He convulsed as his seed shot deep in her channel. Luna's hair was like a silk veil, and he buried his face among the soft strands as he exploded and growled out her name.

As his mind and body emptied, he heard the noise. But maybe the banging on his door was really just his heart pounding. He couldn't stop pumping his hips as his orgasm went on and on.

"Keep moving," Luna begged. "So"—she gasped— "close."

No, he would never stop. He felt more heat, more energy, and more lust rising. His orgasm kept flowing. The feeling was unusual, but he wasn't thinking about whether this sex was atypical or not. Luna's nails dug deep into his back. He thrust his hips harder. Deeper.

Rough male hands came out of nowhere.

"What the hell, Gears?"

Someone yanked on his shoulders from behind. He fought like a wild man, but the hands and arms were too strong. Keith was ripping him out of Luna. He could hear Chen-Ning apologizing and muttering something about not watching her.

"Gears," Luna screamed.

Gears pried himself away from Keith. Dizziness hit him violently. He stumbled as his vision became hazy. The room was spinning. Dropping to his knees, he placed a hand on the floor to steady himself. The room, Luna on the bed, Keith all started to blur. His heart pounded harder. Pain tingled up his left arm. There was a ringing in his ears. Voices faded as his forehead hit the hard tiles.

Then there was nothing.

Chapter 4

"A thousand half-loves must be forsaken to take one whole heart home." Rumi~

"Gears died." Mac's voice floated above him. "That was no joke."

"What? When?"

That might have been Brice. If that was Brice, then he had been traded for Luna. She might have been given back to The Originals now. Gears tried to open his eyes. They were not obeying his command. Immediately, he started to assess what was wrong with him. What had Mac just said? He died? That couldn't be correct. He was alive. He was fine. Well, not fine, but absolutely not dead.

"Chen-Ning said he was dead a full five minutes before he was revived. You were busy being tortured by The Originals. Next time pick a better vacation." Mac's voice floated above him. He tried to get his bearings on who was in the room and where. Gears needed to open his eyes and figure out what was going on.

Struggling, he finally wrestled his eyelids open. Sunlight. Maybe that was a mistake. He couldn't seem to get his eyes open any more than slits. His grainy eyeballs looked to his left. Yes. Sunlight was blinking through a window where the drapes had been pulled open, and a breeze made the fabric sway. The light was shining on the navy-blue carpet. This might not be a water base.

"Some vacation," Brice grumbled. "I barely survived."

"We got you out, but what you did to get captured in the first place was bullshit, Brice. We both know it." Mac was sitting at the foot of the bed. "You should've talked to us."

Gears got his eyes more comfortable with the space. Mac had his back to him, and a book was spread out on a blanket next to Gears' feet. Was Mac reading? He'd never seen his friend read in all the years he'd known him. Brice stood in a light wood doorway. The wood looked clean and new. Again, not a water base.

He racked his brain, trying to remember leaving the base. He also didn't recall dying or being brought back to life. About a hundred questions ran through his head. He needed to ask Mac what had happened. Once he got details, he could work on his health. First, he needed to know what medication he was on and how his heart was doing. Did he have brain damage from his heart stopping? Blood tests might give him additional information, once he could get up out of bed.

A monitor beeped near his head. What exams had Doctor Dana performed while he was sleeping? He would want to look at all the paperwork and documentation. He hoped he was with Dana and not some random doctor who didn't know which way a stethoscope pointed.

Brice and Mac had fallen strangely silent. Gears' eyes flipped to Mac again. Mac got up from where he was sitting. He meandered to the window, crossed his arms over his massive chest, then stared into the light. Brice picked up the book he'd left on the bed and began to page through it. The title on the cover read *Romeo and Juliet*.

This didn't feel right. Where was the sense of urgency that was always hanging around Mac? His long-time friend wasn't barking commands or... being with Karma.

Karma. Where was she? Where was the baby? Mac was going to take time off. Why was he just standing around Gears' bedroom? A sense of foreboding was filling him. Something was wrong. He had to ask what was the matter.

Gears' tongue licked the seam of his lips. One question at a time.

"Where am I?" Gears turned his head and spotted his glasses on the bedside table.

Brice and Mac turned to look at him at the same time. Mac's eyes got enormous. Brice took a step toward the bed, then shook his head, then took a step toward the door.

"Should I call a doctor?" Brice asked, taking another single step toward him. He seemed highly confused. Gears had no idea why.

"I am a doctor." Gears tried to sit up, but his muscles ached. His arm lifted, then fell back on the bed. "Where am I?" he tried again.

"Call Dana right away," Mac commanded. He snatched the book out of Brice's hand, then shoved him toward the door. Mac turned to Gears and threw the book down on the bedside table, making his glasses bounce. This was more like his friend.

"Damn you, Gears. If you ever scare me like that again, I'll kill you myself." Mac came closer to the bed. Then, to Gears' surprise, he leaned down and gently wrapped his massive, meaty arms around his shoulders. He squeezed him briefly before leaning away from him.

Were those tears in Mac's eyes? Did Mac just hug him? His friend picked up Gears' hand and held it.

What was wrong? Mac never did things like this.

"Is the baby okay?"

"The baby is perfect." A grin split Mac's face. "Leave it to you to worry about that."

"Is Karma okay?" Gears was truly puzzled now.

"Karma is on our water base with Keith and the baby. It's just Brice, Chen, and me." Mac paused. "And Doctor Dana."

Mac's eyes were slowly turning into a glare. Dana must have told him. He braced himself for Mac's fury.

"Dana told you about my heart?" Gears didn't wait for an answer. "He shouldn't have. That was not his information to give."

"I would've beat it out of him. But you should've told me. We're friends. I shouldn't have found out when you died." He let go of his hand and picked up Gears' glasses. He helped to perch them on his nose.

A long pause stretched between them.

"I died? Are you sure?" Gears couldn't help being skeptical. He had fallen asleep, last he recalled.

"Yes, I'm sure. I'm not a moron." Mac spun away from him to return to lounging in front of the window. "You don't remember, do you?" he added flatly as he crossed his arms over his chest.

"When?"

"Do you remember delivering my baby?"

"Yes."

"Do you remember a woman named Luna?"

Gears frowned. Yes, he recalled Luna. He was pretty sure if he closed his eyes he could still taste her on his lips. He nodded and waited to see what Mac was going to say.

"Keith and Chen caught you having sex with her. When they told me, I didn't believe it. You know the rules about prisoners, and I said you weren't like that anyway. They claimed she was scratching your back to get you off of her. They pried you away from her and told me you were crazed. Chen said he'd never seen you like that."

"He told me you were possessed by the devil," Dana said as he came into the doorway. "He asked me if I could do an exorcism." He crossed the room and lifted Gears' hand. "I'm glad to see you awake, Doctor Gears."

"Just Gears." He gathered his energy to pry his hand out of Dana's grip. It only flopped on the bed. Dana fiddled with a plastic monitor on his finger.

"After you were pulled off Luna," Mac turned and leaned against the windowsill, "you died. Chen and Keith told me you had no pulse. It was Chen who ran for Dana."

"So, Dana saved me?" Gears asked. He really didn't like the other doctor, but he was man enough to thank him for saving his life. "Thank you."

The whole story sounded unbelievable, yet he did recall the sex, and there had been something inside of him that had broken free that day. Maybe he was crazed. Mac wouldn't lie to him.

"No need to thank me. I couldn't bring you back." Dana was reading a screen behind him. On a chart, he was jotting down notes. Gears would need to see his records. "Luna asked Keith if she could do it. He let her go long enough to… well…" Dana paused. "I don't know what she did, but she got your heart beating again."

This was a lot to process. So, Luna had brought him back from the grave. Why? She was with The Originals. The sex kept replaying in his mind. Had she been fighting him off? He didn't remember that, but they were right. He wasn't acting like himself that day. He had been filled with lust. Not just filled; the desire for Luna had overflowed into his entire being. He'd been drowning in it. He didn't know how else to describe what had happened.

"I don't know what to say." Gears' eyes went to Mac. So much of the situation was foggy. He just needed a minute to get his gears to start turning. Then he would have it all figured out in no time.

"That's a first," Mac muttered.

"You can't have sex with your heart condition," Dana said, more to a file he held than to Gears.

"I don't know what happened with Luna." Gears succeeded in lifting his hand. He pushed up his glasses. "I know that I have a serious heart problem."

"Do you?" Mac bit out. "Coz' you didn't share that with me."

"I didn't want you to worry. And I still don't want you to. Your baby is a few days old, Mac. That should be your only concern."

"I'll argue that." Mac shook his head.

"You're going to worry about me no matter what I say, aren't you?"

"Yes, but also my baby is a month old today."

Gears' eyes jumped from Mac to Dana for confirmation. That had to be wrong. It *had* to be.

"You've been in a coma for about thirty days, Doctor Gears." Dana held up his file so Gears could clearly read the date.

Chapter 5

"Patience is not sitting and waiting, it is foreseeing. It is looking at the night and seeing the day. Lovers are patient and know that the moon needs time to become full." Rumi~

According to the calendar that hung next to Gears' window, today was exactly one year since he'd woken up from his coma. One year of receiving nonsensical letters from Luna. One year of living in the H.S.P.C. Headquarters under Dana's thumb, and one year of getting absolutely nothing accomplished.

His life had become a waste.

Gears raised his hand to rip the calendar off the wall. The action was draining, and instead of clutching the stapled paper, he placed his hand on the wall for support. He took a deep breath, then slumped next to the pushpin. Every day his heart weakened. His brain barely functioned anymore. He was too tired to work, think, or move. He couldn't stop his life from crumbling around him no matter how hard he tried. He still had no answers.

The dawn was approaching. The gentle rise of the sun filled his view as he stood in front of the lone window on the far side of his room. The sun made him think of Luna. The only bright spot in his life right now was the silly messages she sent him. He read every word she wrote. He hung on every one of her Rumi quotes. There was no reason why he still felt connected to her, but she said it was the universe. After a year, it had become easier to just agree with her than have an imaginary argument with her in his head.

Walking away from the window, Gears picked up the copy of *Romeo and Juliet* that was sitting on his bedside table next to a pile of old medical records he was reading. Luna had sent this book to him right after he'd been brought to Dallas. That had been right before she'd been handed over to Hunter. Luna had sent the copy with the same messenger who brought all the letters. Placing the book back down next to an uneaten tray of dried food, he slowly reached for his cane and shuffled over to his sink.

After splashing water on his face and brushing his teeth, he looked at his gray complexion and his day's growth of beard. Shaving wasn't going to happen today. Maybe not tomorrow, either. If only he knew of a way to send Luna a note back. Gears wanted to tell her goodbye. He wasn't going to keep living, he could see that. Even now, he was on borrowed time, and he wanted to tell her that her letters, though confusing, were the only highlight in his life. He would wish her all the happiness in the world and thank her for bringing him back from the grave. Even if he couldn't survive, he still wanted to thank her for trying to help him.

The door to his room opened slightly. Chen-Ning's head darted into view.

"Hey, old man." Chen-Ning waited for Gears to wave him into the room before entering. The young guard hadn't returned to their water base after accompanying Mac here. Gears thought Chen-Ning had decided to stay at HQ because he assumed everyone would be nicer to him. Chen-Ning was probably hoping he wouldn't be such an outcast in Dallas. He was wrong, but he had stayed. Due to the fact that no one else seemed to be able to put up with him for longer than twenty minutes, Chen-Ning spent a ridiculous amount of time with Gears. Honestly, it didn't really matter. The now twenty-year-old was irritating, but he was kind-hearted deep down, and sometimes it was nice to not be alone.

"You're early this morning." Gears placed a handful of strong prescription medication in his mouth, then sipped on some water, forcing the tablets down.

"What do you care?" Chen-Ning leaned in the doorway. "You never sleep anymore."

"I won't argue." Gears pushed up his glasses. He rarely slept, and when he did it was drug-induced.

"If you're going to do all that pill popping around me, the least you could do is share the fun." Chen-Ning shoved his hands into the pockets of his cargo pants as he strolled further into the room.

"You're grating enough sober. I'd hate to hear what you'd say if you were intoxicated." Gears gathered up the rest of his medications then set his water glass down next to a handful of scattered label makers Mac had brought during his last visit.

"You're crabby today, old man. I thought maybe you'd want to go downstairs and see if you have any more messages from your secret admirer." Chen-Ning grinned at him. "We could also troll for someone to bone."

"No, thank you. I'm not interested in boning." Gears' eyes went to the rubber-banded stack of notes from Luna. "We can go down and get my messages, however."

Chen-Ning shrugged, then wandered over to the window while Gears combed his shaggy hair. If he was going to collect his notes, he might as well try to look at least a little bit presentable.

When he was done taming his hair, Gears picked up the letters and shoved them into his backpack. No one knew the messages came from Luna. She only drew a picture of the moon on the bottom of the notes. In the beginning, Gears had sent a few H.S.P.C. agents to follow the young child that Luna had been using as a courier, in case he could find her again. The project had been unsuccessful, a rare occurrence, since Gears generally accomplished whatever he put his mind to. The men came back telling him that the kid had vanished into the crowd. Gears never pursued it after that. He was afraid that his inquiries would draw questions he didn't want to answer.

"I'll get my sweater."

"I'll get it." Chen-Ning crossed to his cabinet and removed a blue button-up cardigan. "I don't have forty-five years to wait while you grab it." He walked back to Gears and helped him put it on. "Here's your I'm-an-old-man sweater."

"I don't recall asking you for fashion advice," Gears muttered.

"It's just a perk of hanging out with me."

These were the moments Gears hated the most. He felt like a baby. He was always out of breath, and doing simple things like putting on his sweater was now difficult without assistance. The banter with Chen-Ning helped a little to lessen the sting of being helpless.

"Thank you, Chen-Ning." While the young man finished buttoning the front, Gears tried to come up with a topic to make the motherly action less awkward. "Where's Egon today? Are you going to see him after you help me get my messages?"

Chen-Ning finished with the bottom button before looking up.

"Egon dumped me. He's an asshole. That's how those German guys are."

"That's what you said about the Asian guys, the Irish guys, and the Hispanic guys."

"Just goes to show I'm not racist. All men are assholes."

"If you are irritated with every rub, how will you be polished?" In Gears' estimation, Egon had been Chen-Ning's seventh boyfriend in the last four weeks. Right now, he couldn't solve his heart problems, but at a minimum he could use his remaining days to help Chen-Ning become at least a little more enlightened.

"Are you offering to rub me?" Chen-Ning smiled. "Feeling sexy this morning?"

"I'm not going to answer that." Gears sighed. "What happened?" Gears leaned on Chen-Ning's arm after the guard lifted his backpack and placed it on his shoulders.

"I think he was only dating me to get me to do his guard duty for him." Chen-Ning shrugged as they left his room and stepped out into the quiet carpeted hallway. "The sex wasn't even good. He just kind of flopped around on top of me." The door closed behind them with a hushed click.

"Please, for the love of God, no more description." Gears leaned on his cane as Chen-Ning steered them down the hall. "Were you doing his work for him?"

"Yes, but when there wasn't anyone in holding it was bye-bye Chen." They turned the corner. Up ahead was a small sitting area next to the set of elevators. Since it was relatively early in the morning no one was waiting.

"I'm sorry, Chen."

"I'm not. At least I keep trying. I'm getting involved." Chen gave him a pointed look.

"Don't start with that." Gears stopped shuffling his feet and held up his cane in front of the guard's face. "Look at me. Do I look like someone who can get involved?" This wasn't the first occasion Chen-Ning had mentioned that he thought Gears had given up. The young man didn't understand. Gears had tried, but his brain abandoned him. His heart, his soul, and his love of learning and life were all gone. He couldn't get it back. His world was ending. Work used to be his everything. Now, without anything to strive for, he had nothing left. He was nothing but a shell.

"You can either start living or start dying." Chen-Ning tugged him along, forcing Gears to lean on his cane once more. There was just no getting through to Chen-Ning.

"I'll pick the second option."

"Don't say that, old man."

"You know I'm not old. I'm not even thirty-five yet." Gears wished Chen-Ning would stop calling him "old man", but no matter how many times he corrected him, he kept on with the nickname. Gears should've given up by this point.

"You're just good at fooling me, then."

They reached the elevator. As they waited, the chime dinged to signify the lift was on their floor. Chen-Ning sighed as he watched the numbers that lit up above the doorway. That mournful sigh made Gears feel sorry for him. The young man was just trying to help. Even his term "old man" was just his way of showing his affection.

"Do you want this 'old man' to give you some advice?"

"No, thanks. Maybe I should be like you and just sit in my room all day, not eating or sleeping. I'm never going to meet someone who likes me." Chen-Ning spoke to the doors that opened. "I piss everyone off."

"Rumi says 'You have to keep breaking your heart until it opens.'" Gears pushed up his glasses.

"That's depressing."

"You're going to meet someone great one day. Someone who likes what you have to say," Gears assured him as he shuffled onto the elevator. "I promise."

"I hope so." Chen-Ning stepped inside after him and leaned against the wall near the buttons. "Joke's on Egon anyway. There's someone back in holding. Of course, I heard he got Essie to cover the shift for him."

"Essie isn't a fool. If he's there, it's because he wants to be there."

"Maybe. I heard it's a pretty woman. They said she's crazy, though. Pretty or not, I didn't want to be a part of that again."

The word "again" struck Gears. Luna. Good heavens, was she the woman they had here? What if she had come back? Her letters didn't say anything about returning, but then again, he didn't know what she was talking about fifty percent of the time.

"Who's in holding? What's the woman's name?" Gears' heart began to pound. Something inside of him nagged that she was here.

"I don't know." Chen-Ning tipped his head to the side and regarded him. "Are you okay?" Chen-Ning patted his back. "You look even more shitty than normal."

"I'd like to speak with Essie." Gears pushed up his glasses. "And telling someone they look bad isn't a nice thing to say."

"I didn't say bad, I said shitty." The guard shrugged.

"Just take me to Essie."

"Why?" Chen-Ning gave him a second sideways look. "Is this about him taking Egon's shift?"

"No, don't be absurd. I just have business with him, and now would be the best time, while I'm out of my room. Take me to the holding area."

Chen-Ning shrugged, then pressed the button on the elevator wall.

Even though Gears had spent a lot of time in his room working to solve his heart problem, he still had a fairly firm grasp of the H.S.P.C. building layout. The elevator zipped to floor six, where a guard was waiting behind a tall desk. Gears flashed his badge to the huge man, but the flip of the plastic card wasn't necessary. Everyone in the building knew who he was. In HQ, he was treated with respect, even if they did make a few jokes about him looking and walking like an eighty-year-old man.

Chen-Ning escorted him down the sterile tile hall to a door on the far end. When he paused to knock, Gears shook his head at Chen-Ning and stopped his hand.

"One moment. I need to get something for Essie."

Gears dug in his backpack and found what he was looking for. In a plastic bag tucked into one of the side pockets was a handful of ground-up sleeping pills. Once he opened the bag, he removed a long blue glass pipe from a front pocket. Months ago, he'd planned to give Essie the ornate pipe. He hadn't seen the other man much lately, and this wasn't the way he wanted to give him such a present, but Gears was going to do whatever he had to do if Luna was the one Essie was guarding. He didn't know why he thought she was here, but he felt it. He felt their connection deep in his bones. She was deep within his heart. It was the most unscientific, illogical reaction, but being so close to death he disregarded all his analytical thinking.

"Go ahead and knock." Gears leaned heavily on his cane and shrugged his backpack back onto his shoulder. Chen-Ning nodded and gave a few hard raps on the entrance. The metal door opened with a silent sweep. Essie peeked out at them.

"El medico, what're you doing here?"

"I wanted to give you a gift. I'm running out of time." His eyes speared Essie's.

The other man nodded and gave nothing away. "Time's a funny thing."

"You would know," Gears responded and pushed past him into a small room. "Chen-Ning, please go wait with the other guard. I'll be a few minutes."

"Okay. I'll try out black men." Chen-Ning grinned and disappeared without further prompting.

Gears held his smile as his friend scampered off. Chen-Ning was so transparent when he liked someone. Good. The guard would have a new boyfriend, and he wouldn't be looking for him for a few minutes, at least.

Gears assessed the little six-by-six room while he set his pack on the floor. On one side was the door he had entered and on the other side was another heavy metal door. That door led into an interrogation room.

Essie was watching him intently.

"What are you *really* doing here, Gears?" The shrewd man pinned him with his gaze. Gears wondered what he knew about him and Luna, if anything. He detested lying, but he was going to see if she was on the other side of that door, and Essie wasn't going to stand in his way.

"I brought you this." Gears pulled out the fragile glass pipe. The glaze had swirls of blue and white, and the coating caught the light with a splendid shine. "I got it from a harvester that I took a blood sample from. That was way back when I was still working on Snow Flu. I know I harp at you to quit smoking, but it appears you'll be living longer than I will."

Essie chuckled. "I'm always a little jealous of those who can die." He took the pipe from Gears' hand. "Gracias, Doctor."

Gears turned to the door as if he was going to exit. His heart thumped, but he wasn't sure if it was excitement, fear, or just his condition. Out of the corner of his eye, he saw Essie bring the pipe to his lips. That was Essie. He was going to try the pipe out.

As soon as his lips wrapped around the pipe, he sucked in, then coughed. Essie might be old, but he was human.

"Are you okay?" Gears spun around with fake concern plastered on his face. He patted the other man's back. Essie nodded, then wobbled. "Maybe you should sit for a moment." Gears held out his hand and Essie sank to the floor. His eyes started to close. Perfect.

Quickly, Gears did some math in his head. When he'd tested the drug out on his rabbits, they'd slept for forty-six hours. He did some quick figuring on Essie's size and how much of the sleeping drug he'd ingested.

"No lo haga. Don't do it, Gears," Essie mumbled. The guard tried to pry his eyes open, but they just slipped closed again. "She killed you before."

"She's worth it," Gears answered automatically.

Essie slumped over and his head hit the tiles. The sound of a deep snore filled the tiny room. Well, that answered one question.

Luna was here.

Chapter 6

"You'll never find me. For I have been with you, from the beginning of me." Rumi~

Gears used the set of keys off Essie's sleeping form to open the door. As he inched it open and peered in, his heart missed a beat. Pain shot through his chest and he took a second to catch his breath. His eyes alighted on Luna as soon as the door was open. She sat at a rectangular metal table in the center of a dark gray padded room. Her hair was in stark contrast to the dark décor.

Luna's hands were chained to the table, but she didn't look worried about being restrained. She looked the same as always. Tranquil, beautiful, contemplative. She was probably silently quoting Rumi in her head. He'd learned from her letters that she did that when she was scared or nervous.

Gears opened the door a little more to make room for his cane as he hobbled in. She looked up as soon as he entered.

Their eyes locked, and it was as if no time had passed. He felt exactly the same way he had when he met her for the first time. Her large blue fathomless pools drew him in. He was swimming… drowning.

"You look like you need your Conpar. I came as soon as I could." Luna moved her hand slightly and the chain scraped against the top. She pushed some of her milky hair off her shoulder and along her cream-colored shirt.

Gears shuffled over to the table. His hands were shaking and his chest felt like someone was sitting on him. He unlocked the chain while he tried to get ahold of his mixed emotions. The cuffs slipped off her dainty wrists and she shoved them towards the floor.

"Luna, I don't know why I'm here."

"I know why."

"You do?"

"I'll tell you." A seductive smile danced on her lips as Luna came around the table. She halted in front of him. He could smell her. Just like the last time they'd met, his cock twitched awake. What was he doing? She was going to kill him again. He wasn't thinking straight. "You're here to finish what we started." Her hands went to the bottom of her top.

"You can't be serious. Luna. We can't." But he wanted her with an intensity that was unprecedented. He supposed there were worse ways to die than in the arms of an enchanting witch. He didn't even believe in magic, but he did believe in insanity. Madness was doing the same thing over and over again expecting a different result. He understood that, but he seemed doomed to repeat history.

"Yes, we can." Her fingers tugged at the shirt, and with a graceful sweep she pulled the garment over her head. His heart slammed against his ribs.

Fine. He was going to die anyway. If he was going to depart this world, then he would do it deep inside of a woman he was strangely linked to. Never mind logic and integrity and right and wrong. Forget it all. He let go of his cane and it clattered to the floor. He reached for her.

Luna took both his hands in hers. Her fingers were warm, and heat spread from his palms up his arms then on to his core. A tingling electric shock zapped his body, making him tremble.

"Sit." Luna stepped to the side and guided him to the table. A burst of energy, maybe from seeing her or touching her, infused him. He hopped up on the metal tabletop when she motioned for him to do so. Once he was seated, she stepped in front of him and ran her fingers around the elastic that held up her floor-length skirt.

"I wanted to thank you for your letters." His eyes jumped from her hands on her waist up to her bra. The fabric was white, and it made her skin look like a ripe peach.

"I like sharing with you, my match." She tilted her head. "Are you ready?"

Gears drank in the sight of her. This might be the last thing he would see, and the view was amazing. She was maybe the only thing he would ever want to look at.

"I'm ready." He pushed up his glasses.

Luna tossed some of the silky length of her hair over her shoulder and arched an eyebrow.

"Watch me, my healer, and awaken all your dormant energy. Don't hold back."

Gears nodded. He didn't know exactly what that meant, but he didn't care anymore. Placing his hands on either side of him, he simply waited.

Luna grinned at him, then turned around. With her back to him, she kicked off her shoes. Her slim fingers came into view as she unclasped her bra. He noted the four fingers on her hand, and the smooth skin still awed him. He didn't have time to think about the missing phalange. The scrap of white fabric fell to the floor. Gears' eyes followed her spine and the smooth lines of her back.

Her hands went to the waist of her skirt again. The bottom of the skirt fanned out slightly when she pushed down. Then the clothing was on the floor and he was staring at the backside of a completely nude Luna.

Gears' cock went hard in an instant. It strained against the fly of his jeans.

"No underwear." Luna smiled over her shoulder. "I remembered."

Gears chuckled. Then his smile disappeared as his jaw dropped.

Luna spun around and lifted her arms up above her head. She mumbled something with her eyes closed, and her hips twisted and undulated.

"I'm channeling more energy for you." She swayed and danced closer to him. When she was directly in front of him, she reached out and spread his legs so she could rock her hips back and forth as if she could hear music.

"What?"

"Shh." Luna put her fingers on his lips. The tips of her fingers moved from his mouth to slip over her bare flesh. "Don't say 'what' right now."

His hands gripped tightly to the edge of the table as he stared at her, mesmerized. Spellbound was the only word he could think of that fit this moment. His cock swelled further as her fingers disappeared between the folds of her slit. He'd never been this aroused in his life.

Only Luna seemed to be able to do this to him. As she spread her legs and twirled around, he was positive he could smell her heat. He ruthlessly held on to his control. He wanted to grab her, bend her over, then slide into her channel. No. He would hold the desire in. He would wait.

Suddenly she stopped and spun around to face him. Both her hands went straight to the buttons on his sweater. She slipped each of them through the holes. When the shirt was loose, she slipped the fabric off his shoulders. Gears let go of the table to help her. He got the sweater off, then right away he yanked off his shirt. Luna's hands spread wide over his heart.

Her eyes were like a gleaming pool of clear water. Hips still swaying, she was silently calling to him. A primal fire burned under her palms.

"Do you feel it?"

"Good heavens." His chest prickled. "I feel it."

"Yes. Feel." Her hips undulated as she glided across the gray tiles a few steps back from him. "Submit to love…"

"…without thinking." He finished the Rumi quote.

When she came nearer, he expected her hands on his chest a second time. Instead, she placed her fingertips on his shoulders. She threw her head back and her lithe body arched, thrusting her breasts out. He held on to the table again.

Gears was so busy being hypnotized by her pink nipples that he barely noticed when she brought her thigh up next to his. He leaned back as she mounted the table in one easy motion. She startled him, and her rising to straddle his lap forced him to lean back on his elbows. Tipping her head to the side, she flashed him a dazzling smile. The room melted away and there was only the two of them.

Her fingers danced over his chest and stomach. Every muscle in his body became stiff when her fingers fluttered over the length of his fly. She toyed with his hard cock through the fabric of his jeans, and a growl escaped his lips.

"Gears," she murmured. "Don't hold back." Luna eased his zipper down until his dick sprang into her waiting palms. His hips jerked. Gritting his teeth, his fought for control. His whole body tried to climb into her hands. She rose then seated herself down on his hard erection. He slid into her slick channel like they would always fit together.

"Luna." His voice was breathless. His heart pounded. "You're worth dying for."

Luna grinned. "I'm worth living for." She tilted her head back and rocked her hips only slightly. Her gaze burned into him. She dipped her head and flicked her tongue along his lips.

Gears' heartbeat roared in his ears. He gripped whatever he could to keep from reaching for her and driving into her warmth like a wild animal.

Luna must have noticed his hands. Her fingers ran down his arms and over his white knuckles.

"My eyes are open. I know I'm with you. Let go and touch me."

Gears gave in. He cupped his hands around her cheeks, loving the silky texture of her ass.

Rising up, he pressed his naked chest to hers. His mouth started at her neck then began to work its way down to her nipples. He caught one of her stiff peaks between his teeth. Luna's breathing hitched. He sucked the tight, pebbled flesh deep into his mouth as his hands ran up and down her smooth back. Sucking the flesh into his mouth harder, he worked his tongue over the tip and felt her pussy tighten with every tug. A moan escaped her. The sound washed through and around him and echoed off the empty walls.

Their combined scent filled his nostrils. Her wetness and the smell of sex were like a drug. He couldn't think. He could only feel.

"Ride me," Gears demanded. He didn't even know where that came from, but she did as he commanded.

Luna's hips rocked harder. She ground down on him. The muscles in her thighs clenched on his hips as she moved on him. Her slick flesh gripped him more firmly as he tried to hold back his climax. He wanted to savor her. He wasn't ready to let this end. Good heavens, he wasn't ready to let his life end either. He only wanted more and more of her.

Using his hands, he pushed her down roughly on his shaft. His thumb rubbed against her clit. He rolled his hips, shoving himself deeper into her core. Luna cried out as she arched her body against his. As she rode him, she kept her eyes on him just like the first time. Her eyes were still that same indescribable blue. She wouldn't stop watching him, and deep down he loved that she was there with him, just as eager. Her nails scraped against his forearms and she moaned louder.

As they began to move together faster and rougher, the creak of the table became music. The slap of flesh on flesh was like the beat of a tribal drum. Luna bent her head and her tongue slid around his collarbone until her lips closed over the skin of his neck. She sucked on his flesh and his cock swelled and throbbed inside of her. He would never want more than this. All his dreams, living, dying, curing Snow Flu, none of it mattered. Luna mattered.

"I think I love you." His fingers clenched into her hips and his breathing became harsh. "Conpar."

Luna nipped at his skin, then lifted her head. Slapping both hands over his chest, she pressed him flat again the metal top. Raising her hips up, she started to grind down on him brutally. He couldn't take the intense pleasure. His cock glided into her with increasing speed. The tempo built his climax without his consent. Luna wouldn't slow.

A roar of satisfaction, one that he didn't even know he had inside of him, sliced through the room. His body locked and she ground onto his pelvis. He became a hard line that she continued to ride as he jetted his load deep into her center. The hot walls of her channel fisted around him then milked him mercilessly.

Luna screamed as she shuddered. Tremors racked her body. Her arms wrapped tightly around his neck, sealing their bodies together.

Her orgasm electrified him. Shockwaves rolled through his body and he quivered while she held him immobile. Again, the sensations seemed to go on forever.

When he could finally move, he was a little afraid his heart wouldn't be able to take it. He groaned. She lifted her head slightly and looked down at him.

"You look better already." Her breath cooled the sweat on his skin as she panted. His muscles shook in the aftermath. That might have been the most intense orgasm of his entire life. He closed his eyes as he rested his head on the table. Luna placed her head on his chest over his heart as if she was listening to the beat. His fingers wound through the silky mass of her hair.

"Chen-Ning said I looked… well, he used a crude word, but basically he said I looked bad."

"You always look beautiful to me. Your soul is breathtaking," Luna murmured into his chest. "But yes, your skin has a healthier glow now."

Gears' chest felt tight, but there was no pain. It was more like he couldn't hold in all the gratitude of having Luna back in his arms. *Thank you, God.* Only in his wildest dreams had he ever thought to be with her again, especially like this. And his heartbeat had a strong, steady rhythm. He took a deep breath. She saved him.

"You healed me." Wonder and reverence for what she had done for him surged through him. She was exceptionally powerful, although he had no idea how she did it. He felt amazing. If he wanted to, he could probably run right now. He hadn't run in a long time. Except that he had just run from death's door. Luna was his savior, his mystic, his match.

"Yes." Luna sat up. "You feel better?"

"Yes." His softening penis slipped from her wet sex.

Luna lifted herself off of his body then stood. Good Heavens, he'd just had sex in an interrogation room. On a table. What was he thinking?

Gears scooted to the end of the table, then rose. He braced himself for the dizziness or the exhaustion that had been his constant companion this last year. Neither came. He felt fantastic.

Reaching down, he pulled up his pants before he picked up Luna's shirt. He had to get her dressed then smuggle her out of here. He had to find out where she was going, and a part of him demanded that wherever she go, he follow. Was he really considering leaving H.S.P.C. for her? Yes, that was exactly what he was deliberating right now.

Luna was snapping her bra closed when their eyes met. She smiled. He handed her the top he was holding and pulled on his shirt and sweater as she tugged on her shoes.

"May we go now?" She asked him when the last of his buttons were through the loops.

"You want me to come with you?" Here it was. She was going to ask him to leave. He didn't feel prepared for the question. What about Mac? He would miss his best friend. Even though they didn't see each other as much as before, Mac still visited him often. His friend liked to bring him label makers. They talked and wrote. His heart hurt just thinking about it.

"You have to come with me." Luna tipped her head to the side, puzzled. "I told you in my letter that I need your assistance to get Archer. I thought you'd want to help."

Immediately, Gears closed his eyes and recalled every word she had wrote to him. Yes, he remembered her mentioning Archer. Something about being surprised when he arrived, and enjoying his company. For the hundredth time, Gears felt he needed a manual to understand Luna.

"Who's Archer again?"

She never told him to begin with who Archer was exactly, but he presumed he would figure it out eventually.

Luna shook her head at him like he had just asked a trivial question. She reached for the door.

"Archer is your son. I want him to live here with you."

Chapter 7

"Set your life on fire. Seek those who fan your flames." Rumi~

There had been women before Luna who tried to get entangled with him because they thought he had control over the water bases. Normally, he could see straight through a woman who was using him. But this? This he had no idea if Luna was messing with him to escape. He would've helped her no matter what. She didn't need to lie to him.

Gears unzipped Essie's hooded sweatshirt.

"You don't look like you had a baby." He wiggled Essie's sleeping form out of the top, then turned to look up at Luna. "You don't need to make up a lie to get me to help you. For some unknown reason, I seem to be incapable of *not* helping you. God knows, I've tried to leave you be." Gears stood. "I'm here for you."

"I can heal myself as well as others." She took the huge sweater and pulled her arms through the sleeves. As she bent over to tie her sneakers, her skirt hugged her ass like a lover. Gears stopped himself from groaning. "Archer came and I just put myself back to the way I was. Are you disappointed that we have a child together?"

"Disappointed? No, I'm furious." Reaching over to her, he angrily zipped Essie's hoodie up and stopped himself from shaking her. This news infuriated him. A strong emotion like this was such a rare occurrence that he almost didn't know what to do. Then his brain kicked on. "Why didn't you make it clear we had a baby? You should've written 'We have a child and his name is Archer.' Sweet heavens, Luna!" He gripped her shoulders, digging his fingers into the soft fabric.

"Getting the letters to you was hard enough, and I didn't know who might read them." Luna's answer placated him a small amount, but he was still upset. She looked down at the sweatshirt and hugged the fabric to her body.

"I have a baby out there somewhere and I didn't even know." Gears let go of her and prowled the room.

"You don't want children?" Luna wouldn't look at him. "I had hoped you'd want him."

He hated seeing her so dejected, and that wasn't true. He did want children. In one smooth motion, he lifted his backpack from the floor and settled the straps on his shoulders.

"I want kids." He took her hands and held them, pressing his lips to her fingertips. He then pulled the hood up over her hair. "I want to live a long life, and I wanted to see my child being born. Maybe even deliver him. Up to about a few hours ago, that all seemed impossible." He couldn't very well stay upset at a woman who'd saved his life. Twice! He would think about his child later. They needed to escape first. Once they were free, he could get more details on both Luna and Archer.

"I can't wait for you to meet him." Luna tipped her head forward and sipped at his lips. He stopped her from letting the kiss get out of hand. She was a disruptive element, to say the least. He could be stripping the clothes right back off her.

"None of that now. We have to get out of here." Gears pulled away from her reluctantly and let go of her hands. "We'll talk about Archer later. First, we have to get out of here."

After unlocking the exit door, Gears peeked his head out. He didn't see any guards patrolling the halls. The tension in his shoulders relaxed a little. He linked his fingers through Luna's and stepped out of the interrogation room. As they walked, he handed her Essie's plastic badge.

"Now what?" Luna glanced at Essie's picture on the front of the card.

"That key card will open all the elevators. Just wave it in front of the sensor. If you and I get separated, this, I pray, will help you get out. Right now, you'll have to wait while I handle the watchman by the door. I'll signal to you when you can move to the elevator."

Luna nodded.

At the end of the hall, he spotted Chen-Ning draped over a tall desk. His friend was giving a fake laugh at a rugged looking guard who was tilted backward in a plush office chair. The beefy security guard was rolling his eyes at the ceiling, but that was pretty usual for anyone who had talked to Chen-Ning for longer than five minutes.

Gears made sure Luna was hidden in a doorway at the end of the corridor. He dragged a large potted plant next to her and had her crouch before he headed straight for Chen-Ning.

He prayed.

"Chen-Ning," Gears called out. "I don't think you should date a man on the rebound."

Chen-Ning started like a guilty child stealing cookies. He mumbled an excuse of some kind to the other man, who shrugged. The guard gave a polite smile and respectful nod to Gears as he moved next to him. Gears lounged next to the chair, hoping to keep both men's eyes on him. Chen-Ning glared at him like he'd just lost his mind. Maybe he had.

While both men studied him, Gears reached into the side pocket of his bag and wrapped his fingers around a small needle, but didn't pull it out. The shot he currently held in his fist was the newest version of his immobilization drug. It would take this guard down with no problems. A mild stab of guilt hit him, but he steeled himself against the emotion.

"I'm tired. I want to get back to my room." Gears pretended fatigue and put his hand on the back of the sentry's chair as he inched closer. He had to do this, he reminded himself.

"Go on without me," Chen-Ning snapped. "And this isn't a rebound. Who the hell pissed in your cereal?"

"My cereal is just fine, thank you. Let's go."

Chen-Ning gave an exasperated sigh before he spun around. He started to stalk toward the elevator.

"Doc had to pick up an attitude today," Chen-Ning muttered angrily as he stomped away.

As soon as Chen-Ning turned around, Gears brought his hand out to the sitting watchman and set it firmly on the back of the chair next to his head.

"Sorry. I get dizzy," he murmured. The hand with the needle popped out of the bag before the other man even knew what was happening. Gears injected the guard in his neck before he could even call out. The drug took effect immediately. Gears shoved the needle back into his bag then checked the man's pulse. He would be fine, but he'd be sitting in this chair motionless for a few hours.

Out of the corner of his eye, Gears spotted Chen-Ning waiting for the doors to open. He waved his key card and punched the button three times.

Gears smiled and patted the now frozen lookout. "It was nice to meet you."

The guy didn't even blink. Gears said a brief apology to God, then waved to Luna to stay in her spot for a moment longer. He had to think. He would need Chen-Ning if he was going to get out of here. Mac and Karma were scheduled to show up tomorrow. That was bad timing. He would have to lie about where he was going so Mac didn't look for him. He would also need a vehicle. Chen-Ning was the only person he could think of for getting a car. If he left now, he wouldn't have to lie to his best friend. He wouldn't have to say anything if he didn't see him.

Chen-Ning glanced back at him. "So are we going or what?"

Gears nodded. Good, Chen-Ning didn't see anything out of place with the stationary guard next to him. He hurried over to his friend and waited for the elevator doors to open. His eyes flipped back at Luna. Her head peeked around the corner.

"Damn, Doc." Chen-Ning leaned against the wall. His voice dropped to a whisper. "Way to make me look like a loser." He punched again at the button to force the door to open faster. Everyone knew that didn't work. "He liked me, and I bet he had a big dick."

"No, he didn't." Gears faced a pouting Chen-Ning for a second, then distracted, he glanced back at Luna.

"You know how big his dick is? Like turn your head and cough?"

"No, he didn't like you." Gears sighed. "You do know there's this thing in your head called a brain? It will stop you from talking."

"What's the fun in that?"

Gears gave up on this ludicrous conversation. He didn't have time for this topic.

"I need some help."

"Who would want to help you now that you're being such an asshole. See? Not racist. Even the lame white dudes are assholes."

"Chen, will you please listen to me for a moment?"

"Do you need me to hold you up?" Chen-Ning put a hand on his arm. "You forgot your I'm an eighty-year-old-man cane. I bet that guy's dick is as thick as your cane."

"Thank you for the dreadful mental picture." Gears shook his head. Instead of trying to remember where he'd left his now unneeded cane, he tried to come up with a plan for helping Luna escape. "I need you to get me a vehicle."

"Why? Where do you wanna go?"

Gears eyed Chen-Ning's lean young form. He couldn't ask Mac to help him this time. Karma, Keith, and Brice were out of the question as well. He was about to get seriously involved with The Originals. Who was he kidding? It was too late. He was already up to his eyeballs in having sex, and having a baby, with the girlfriend of the head of The Originals. He tried to come up with how to best approach the subject. He had no close friends here. The people here were all simply new guards training before getting placed on a water base. Chen-Ning was it.

"Luna and I are leaving."

"What the fuck?" Chen-Ning asked as Gears motioned to her. She hurried past the plant and reached his side just as the door to the elevator opened.

"We're running away like Romeo and Juliet." Luna pushed back the hood and smiled.

"That's a shitty idea." Chen-Ning stepped into the lift then leaned as far away from Luna as he could get in the small elevator space.

"I don't like your choice of words." Gears and Luna followed the guard as the doors closed. He couldn't argue that it wasn't the best idea he'd ever had. He had such a small understanding of her gift and how it worked, but he was going to help her. He was going to find his son.

"She could kill you again. She's a witch." Chen-Ning reached out and pushed on the neck of Gears' shirt. He exposed a hickey. Gears blushed.

Gears nodded and pushed his glasses up his nose. That could happen. Not to mention that he could get killed trying to find Archer. He didn't even know where they were going yet.

"And," Chen-Ning continued as he let go of his shirt, "the H.S.P.C. is going to string us up for taking a vehicle and freeing a member of The Originals."

"I considered all of the variables." Gears linked his fingers with Luna's. "Are you saying you're not going to help me?"

"No. I'm saying this is a shitty idea, but good job getting involved. You started living, instead of dying."

Chapter 8

"Love said to me, there is nothing that is not me.

Be silent." Rumi~

The vehicle Chen-Ning picked was a partially rusted green four-door with a police push bar bolted to the front end. The words "Ford Focus" were on the back. The H.S.P.C. had installed a lift kit and put on oversized snow tires. Gears didn't comment about the unusual car and instead hopped into the driver's seat.

He was about to lean his head out the window to thank Chen-Ning for getting him the car when the guard scooted into the backseat. Luna gracefully slid into the passenger side.

Gears gripped the wheel. "What are you doing?"

"Look, you can put in a CD!" Luna smiled with pleasure, then pressed a multitude of buttons on the dash. "Can we listen to a CD? I've always wanted to do that." He heard the click of her seatbelt.

"Fine," he nodded to Luna. "Chen." Gears caught the young man's eyes in the rearview mirror. "What do you think you're doing?"

"I'm going with you." Another click of a seatbelt.

"God forbid." Gears glanced around the deserted garage.

"Okay." Chen-Ning's eyes narrowed to slits. "I'll just get out and tell everyone the truth. That you're stealing a member of The Originals out of the H.S.P.C." Chen-Ning reached for the handle and opened the door.

"Got any Rumi quotes for patience?" Gears mumbled to Luna as he turned the key. They were moving before Chen-Ning could get out.

"I didn't know you knew how to drive." Chen-Ning shut the door as soon as Gears pulled out of the rear parking lot behind motor pool.

"I'm real smart. I know a lot of things." Gears hit the main drive that circled around the H.S.P.C. Headquarters building. Before they reached the gravel drive, he pushed Luna down in the seat. Luna giggled as she squished close to the floor. Chen-Ning threw a black blanket over her head. Chen-Ning then put Gears' backpack on the front seat.

The H.S.P.C. campus was substantial, and Chen-Ning helped Gears navigate to the gates connected to the sizeable stone wall surrounding the compound. A flash of his badge and his name was all that was needed to get him outside the gate and into the city. Most of the sentries here knew that he worked on Snow Flu. Gears gave the guard the impression that he was leaving to gather data.

Once outside the H.S.P.C. grounds, they drove slowly past run-down shanties of various shapes and sizes. The occupied structures looked like they were held together only because the termites within the walls held hands. Graffiti was splashed along the sad buildings. Luna's head popped up as they snaked past skyscrapers and people huddled around trash fires.

"Where exactly are we going?" Chen-Ning asked as they kept driving further away from the heart of Dallas.

"Monclova," came Luna's answer. She threw off the blanket and turned to watch the passing scenery.

"In old Mexico?" Gears' heart jumped in surprise. No need to panic. He could figure this out. His eyes went to the gauge for the gas tank. He reviewed road options in his head. He'd studied piles of maps. Snow Flu was big in that area.

"How are we going to cross the border?" Chen-Ning lifted Gears' bag and put it in the seat next to him. "Also, how much gas do we have? Can we even make it that far?" Chen-Ning leaned forward and his face popped between Luna and Gears. "What's in Monclova?" he asked Luna. Then he looked to Gears. "Do you know, Doctor I'm-so-fucking-brilliant?"

Luna pulled the jacket Gears had given her closer to her body and didn't answer. The heater was on. He didn't think she was cold. Maybe she was just feeling sad that she was away from her son. A mother and child's connection was strong. It didn't take a genius to understand the bond.

"There is no border. Mexico and the old United States are all gone. It's all the C.T.O.N.A.," Gears said to fill the silence when Luna didn't answer Chen-Ning.

"I know that." Chen-Ning rolled his eyes. "That's basic schooling, old man."

"He means the border between where the H.S.P.C. is welcome and the areas that are held by The Originals," Luna muttered after a few seconds ticked by.

"I'm armed, but we'd need a whole escort to get that far past Austin." Chen-Ning produced a map.

Gears' eyes flipped briefly to Luna. "Luna's going to get us in."

"The Originals know me. I'm not worried about that," Luna nodded.

"I forgot, you're Hunter's girlfriend." Chen-Ning leaned back in his seat, apparently satisfied. Gears could hear the crackle of paper as the guard spread out his map.

"Hunter is not my boyfriend!" She laughed until tears gathered in her eyes. She was back to looking pleased again.

Throwing a sideways glance at Luna, Gears decided he liked it much better when she wasn't frowning and looking concerned. He could solve this puzzle of how to get to Monclova. Even though he wasn't a tough water base guard or an H.S.P.C. agent didn't mean he didn't have skills. He was brilliant, after all. He could figure out a way to get near The Originals and get Archer. He had complete faith in his brain. He wanted her to have complete faith in him as well. He might not look like much, but he was smart. Brains over brawn would win in this instance.

"Luna is the healer to The Originals. She will help us get close to their areas."

"Like Gears is your healer," she added.

"We'll get gas." Gears pushed up his glasses. "I can syphon gas out of the tank from any car I find that runs. If we have to steal it, we will. I don't believe in stealing, but —"

"I don't either." Luna reached for his hand and squeezed his fingers just as the road opened up into an empty highway.

"But," Gears sighed, "we will do what we have to do."

Everyone fell silent for a moment.

"So, what's in Monclova?" Chen-Ning asked. "Why do you even want to get close to The Originals? This isn't a suicide mission, is it?" Chen-Ning held up his backpack. "There aren't explosives in here?" His eyes raked the bag "Is there?"

"My baby," Luna whispered. Gears could hear the pain in her voice.

"Our son," Gears said much louder. He had a son. Joy filled him every time he said it or even thought it. At the end of this he would hold his child.

"Goddamn!" Chen-Ning exclaimed. He set the bag down. "No way."

"God should not damn anything." Gears expertly drove around a few cars that were abandoned on the highway. "The Originals have our child."

Luna smiled. "I want Gears to raise our baby. I want Archer to have knowledge and care. I want him to not have to live moving from place to place like I have to do. He should have a home with his father."

"And his mother." Gears peeked at her out of the corner of his eyes. "We're going to get him and then we're going to live together."

"You and Archer will," Luna stated.

"Yes, with you." Gears glanced in the rearview mirror. Chen-Ning was shaking his head back and forth. Gears wasn't going to give up on the hope that Luna could be with him in some way. How could this all end? He wanted his son, yes, but he wanted her too. There was no way he was going to just let her walk away from him when this was all over.

"I have an obligation to The Originals." Luna looked out the window. "Would you leave the H.S.P.C. or your friends for me?"

Gears pushed his glasses up the bridge of his nose. Leave Mac and Karma? Leave Keith and Brice? He glanced into the backseat. Leave all these men that he had cared for and looked after, just for her?

"Are you asking me to join The Originals?"

"I think that's your ego asking." Luna looked from the passing fields and dead trees to him. "No. I'm not asking you to join The Originals. You couldn't leave the H.S.P.C.

and," She brushed her fingers through her hair. "The Originals would never take you. They'd never trust you. Hunter would try to kill you. You can't live in my world, and," she paused, "I can't live in yours."

"Why can't you live in my world?" He cast a quick glance at her. "Women have been throwing themselves at me because they believed I could give them a safe place to live. They pretend to like me, even love me, just for a chance at a secure, safe, comfortable life. I'm not asking you to love me, Luna, I'm offering you a safe home."

"I love you, and I want nothing from you. I don't want a home. I have a place." Luna gave him a warm smile. "I care for those men. I'm a healer. It's in my blood. I care for The Originals. Some of those people are my friends. I'm asking for you to love me the way I am. Help me get Archer and then—"

"And then what? Never see you again?" Gears couldn't keep the frustration out of his voice. That was new.

"We can't plan the future. We can only live for right now. Rumi says 'This moment is all there is.'"

"I'm not agreeing to this." Anger rose, an emotion he was getting more familiar with. Screw the Rumi quotes. He was going to start problem solving for whatever came their way. He took a deep breath. First, he would figure out how to get to Monclova with one tank of gas in a Ford Focus. Then get Archer, then get Luna to come home with him so they could be together. One problem at a time.

"I don't have any answers for you." Luna's lips trembled. "For either of us." She was scared. He could tell by the way she hunched her shoulders and curled into herself.

"Don't worry, Conpar. You mean the world to me. I'm going to figure all this out. I know I don't look like much, but I have brain power. I can get this all solved. You came to me for my help. Now I'm going to help you."

"I trust you, my match." Luna tipped her head to the side. Her eyes brightened. "I only wish we'd have more time together. However, no matter how short or long our moments are, I'll savor every second with you."

"We have a long drive." Gears smiled. He would cherish every moment with her as well, all the way until he died. "Even though I don't understand half of what you say, do you want to talk? Would you like to tell me some Rumi quotes for a while? Or that thing about Mondo Zen meditation and how my chakras should be aligned?"

"I'm glad that you pay such close attention to me," Luna laughed. "But how about you talk instead? Tell me about you."

"Great." From the backseat, Chen-Ning groaned. "He'll tell you all about some weird experiment he's working on, or a stupid animal that he once had." Chen-Ning paused, and his head popped forward again. "You know he has a bizarre love affair with label makers. I think he sleeps with them."

"I noticed the label makers in his bag." Luna's eyes danced.

"What do you want to know?" Gears pointedly ignored Chen-Ning.

Luna didn't answer. She sat up straighter in her seat. Gears did the same thing. He saw what she saw. Up ahead, it looked like a pile of cars were in the middle of the road.

"What is that?" A handful of shattered buildings were on both sides of them, but not many. He could see a car moving in the distance to the left. It looked like a minivan came out of a metal hut then weaved as it sped toward them.

"Pirates." Luna gripped her seatbelt and held it to her chest.

"Pirates?" Gears noted a second minivan that just pulled out of a garage to his right. "As in a person or group of people who attacks and robs ships at sea?"

"More like they attack and rob H.S.P.C. vehicles. Especially when they're all alone." Chen-Ning glanced out the back window. "What should we do?"

"Drive as fast as you can," Luna said simply. "Don't slow down."

"I can do that." Gears pressed the gas pedal all the way to the floor. As he came up on the barricade of cars, he headed for the shoulder. He hit the ditch and the huge tires on the Focus had them bouncing around in the cab. He held on to the wheel until his hands started to ache and skirted around a beat-up Mustang just as another minivan came out of nowhere. He dodged the other vehicle and drove over a few saplings that were growing on the side of the road.

"Poor trees." Luna leaned her head toward the window.

"Poor us." Chen-Ning gripped the handle attached to the ceiling.

Gears got the compact car back up on to the road. In the mirror, three minivans were chasing them.

"They must be carrying cargo." Luna turned her head to look out the back window. "They aren't catching up. We'll be okay. Just don't slow down."

Gunfire split the air and Gears changed lanes while he prayed to God that they didn't hit one of his tires. As soon as an opportunity presented itself to get off this road, he would take it. He sped toward another set of abandoned cars in a pileup. He would have to go around the second obstruction. More gunfire sounded.

"I'll shoot out their tires." Chen-Ning rolled down his window and tried to take aim just as Gears hit the ditch again. Chen-Ning's swearing had Gears missing Mac's more serious shooting and Karma's steady aim.

After passing the broken-down cars, Gears got their car back up on the pavement again. Cars and trucks were littered along the highway up ahead. He raced toward a small, rusted lightweight truck that was askew on the roadway. Aiming for the bumper, he hit the gas and struck the front end. The beat-up truck spun out into the road, coughing up dirt from the shoulder, and rust decorated the road behind him. One of minivans jerked to dodge the vehicle and Gears thanked the heavens when he saw the van slow down.

Weaving in and out of the other abandoned cars, he debated if the Focus could take another hit like that. He could aim for another car when one of the vans got close again.

Just as he saw a second set of cars ahead, the sky opened up.

The clouds above them were always gray with snow, but he hadn't expected bad weather when they first started out. Snow would've been something he could handle. Unfortunately, what was now coming down was a sheet of rain. Water fell in waves, and it was as if the sky had chosen that moment to drop the ocean on them.

The wall of water he drove through was quickly turning into slush, then ice. Gears forgot about the pirates. He used every ability he had to keep the car on the road.

He hydroplaned and pumped his brakes.

"Don't slow down!" Chen-Ning barked.

"I have to." Gears could barely see. The water came down so hard that the wipers couldn't keep the windshield clear. He strained to see ahead of him. If he could just get through the sudden storm, then they would be alright.

He gripped the wheel until his knuckles turned white and leaned forward as if being six inches closer to the dash could improve his visibility. His heart was pounding, and adrenaline washed through his veins. The road started to bend. Just as he took the curve, he saw a minivan ahead of him. The vehicle was driving straight for him.

Gears made the split-second decision to go off-roading again. He had great traction with the snow tires. If he was lucky, these pirates would have bald tires. Since they were lower to the ground, bushes and plants would slow them down. They dipped back into the ditch, then sped toward more ominous thunder.

"I think we're losing them!" Chen-Ning cheered from the back seat. Up ahead, water was making what could either be a large puddle or a small pond. Turing the wheel, Gears maneuvered the car away from the growing pool and saw another road. He had just gotten the tires up on the tar when the car hydroplaned a second time then started to slide. Holding the wheel as steady as possible, he prayed the Focus wouldn't tip. With the huge wheels, he half expected it to roll over. Luna grabbed his hand as they spun off the road and came to a halt on the side of the asphalt.

When their car finally came to rest, Gears let out a long breath.

"Anyone hurt?" Luna asked.

"No," Chen-Ning and he responded in unison.

The water kept coming down in sheets. He let go of Luna's hand. He would have to try to drive out of the ditch and get back up onto the road.

Before he even had his hand on the wheel again, the driver's side door opened suddenly. Standing drenched in rain was a large man in a soaking wet green poncho.

Gears looked up at the angry henchmen getting doused. The sound of the rain made a roaring sound. Gears guessed that the cold water probably wasn't improving the stranger's mood.

"Get out!" The pirate yelled over the rain.

"Is this getting involved enough for you, Chen?" Gears asked just as the man grabbed him by the front of his shirt and heaved him out of the car.

Chapter 9

"In your light I learn how to love." Rumi~

In a book, he had once read the term hogtied. He had thought it applied to animals, hogs specifically. Today he was learning the word didn't have to do with hogs at all.

Gears was tipped on his side with his hands and feet bound together behind him. The pirates had tossed him into the back of the minivan after knotting thick ropes around his wrists and ankles. This wasn't the most comfortable position for problem solving.

His gag had slipped off as soon as he hit the floor of the van. The pirate had tied the knot in a hurry, probably so they could get out of the rain quicker, and the wet fabric fell around his neck almost immediately.

"Luna?' he whispered.

She didn't look too bad for being rained on and captured by pirates. Luna sat next to him with her hands and feet tied together in front of her. She nodded at him, then resumed trying to use her shoulder to push down the gag covering her mouth.

"Chen-Ning?" His voice might not be loud enough for his friend to hear. Beyond the bench seat, was Chen-Ning. The pirates had knocked the guard out before they took his gun, then dumped his unconscious body in the middle of the van. Gears wasn't sure if he was awake yet.

"Got 'em." The door on the driver's side of the van opened. "But we're getting pissed on." Two men grumbled as they took their seats. Doors slammed. Rain continued to pelt the vehicle, making it sound like nails were being hammered into the roof.

Gears struggled to move. His hands could feel a wooden box that was stacked up next to the back hatch. He turned his head over his shoulder and tried to see beyond the water spots on his glasses. Two wooden crates were side by side. The corners of the boxes didn't look sharp enough to cut the ropes. His hand was losing feeling as the thick cord dug in. He wiggled to ease the pins-and-needles feeling. If the boxes couldn't sever the ropes, maybe something else in here could. He glanced around.

The man who took the driver's seat was drying his hair with a towel. Gears wished he could do the same thing. His hair was soaked and plastered to his head. Water was dripping into his eyes. His wet sweater was making his arms itch.

Luna murmured something, then swung her head back and forth trying to dislodge the gag. Apparently, she had given up on using her shoulder for assistance. His eyes wandered to the wet sweater clinging to her skin. In another time and place, he might have enjoyed the way the sopping fabric stretched over her chest, but his miserable state didn't induce desire. Not when he was so cold. He scooted closer to her.

"Luna," he whispered. "It's going to be okay."

Her head moved around and she wiggled closer to him. The rumble of the van's engine drowned out the pirates' conversation. With a lurch, the automobile started moving. Gears rolled even closer to Luna then lifted up to get his face next to hers.

"Stay real still," he whispered. The van's engine sounded more like a rocket ship then a car.

Using his teeth, he yanked the fabric in her mouth downward. The knot on the cloth wasn't much stronger than his had been, and soon the material fell around her neck like a necklace.

Luna's eyes twinkled when the gag was removed. "I always thought it would be sexy for a man to take my clothes off with his teeth. This isn't really what I wanted, though."

Gears raised his eyebrows. "I'll do better next time. One thing about me is, I do learn and adapt."

"I know. You're brilliant." Luna was teasing him, but her comment made him smile. She kissed his cheek.

"Are you hurt at all?"

"I'm not hurt," she whispered. "Just cold."

"Scoot as close to me as you can. I'll try to warm you up." Gears pressed his body to hers as best he could. His movements brought them chest to chest. Her bound hands rubbed his crotch.

"We can't do that right now," Luna giggled into his neck.

Gears shushed her. "I didn't mean 'warm you up' that way."

Luna giggled again, then sobered. "Is Chen alive? They don't normally keep someone who has a gun."

"They knocked him out. He's on the floor in front of the seat." Gears dipped his head, and with his nose closer to the carpet he could see Chen-Ning's bound hands.

"Have they said anything?" Luna asked.

"I only heard the word 'spider' and complaints about the rain."

Luna's eyes widened. "Are you sure you heard the word 'spider'? Are you positive?"

"Yes." Gears didn't like the way her voice shook. She was trembling. He didn't think it had to do with being cold. "That's what I heard." He paused. "Why? Do you think there are spiders in these crates?" Gears quickly threw a glance over his shoulder. It would be okay as long as none of them were venomous. He knew every poisonous spider that had survived the start of the ice era. He wasn't sure how her gift worked as an antivenom.

"It's not the crates. They are going to meet Spider."

"Spider? As in a name?" Gears had heard of Spiderman. "The comic book hero?"

Luna looked pale. She didn't look like they were going to meet a hero of any sort.

"Spider is a trader on the outskirts of Austin." She frowned, but then a slight smile kicked up one side of her face. "It's closer to Monclova, at least."

"Do you think this is a good thing or a bad thing?"

"I don't know. I met him once when traveling with Hunter. Spider comes from a huge Italian family that lives in a gated community in Austin. Him and a few of his siblings all live in this huge mansion. He trades, buys, and sells everything. He has no allegiance to the H.S.P.C. or The Originals."

"How about to pirates?"

"He doesn't like them either, but he'll trade with anyone."

Gears now understood her changing expression. This might be good or bad. It would be hard to tell until they were facing the man.

"So he might not kill us. I'm going to stay positive. I'd say that's a good thing." Gears rolled his shoulder. It was a long way to Austin. They would have to get comfortable in this position. He tried to tug on the ropes behind him. He wished his glasses would stop fogging up.

"I told you, Romeo, we aren't going to die." Luna gave a hushed chuckle toward the floor, then tipped her head onto his shoulder. "But we're going to have to find out some new way to get a car."

"I'll figure out where we can get a car." Already his mind started to work on what he knew about huge Italian families, what were the most valuable items for sale, and what they might they be able to get their hands on. "I wish I could clean my glasses."

"We're going to be okay, right, Gears?" She snuggled into his neck and sighed. His glasses fogged up again, but he smiled.

"I have you, and Chen, and my glasses. We're alive. Everything is going to be just fine."

Surprisingly, with Luna cuddled closer to him he thought that was true. Maybe he could even come up with a way to escape. No matter what happened, he wasn't worried as long as Luna was with him and not hurt.

"I love you." Luna's words made him feel powerful. He would save them. No doubts lingered in his head.

After a moment, Gears thought she might have fallen asleep on his shoulder. "Luna?" He whispered into her shoulder. "Why do they call him Spider? That's not an Italian name."

"Because they say once you're in his web, rarely do you leave."

Chapter 10

"When I am with you, we stay up all night. When you're not here, I can't go to sleep. Praise God for those two insomnias, and the difference between them." Rumi~

His feet and hands had gone numb hours ago, but he was having an enjoyable time talking with Luna. In the back of the van, they discussed everything. Life, their very different worlds, and, of course, strategy. Luna went over everything she knew about The Originals and where they would find Archer in Monclova. After they made plans, she also told him about giving birth and her life with Hunter. Gears got the chance to ask her every question he'd wanted to ask since he met her. She was amazingly smart, and her quiet strength continued to give him the confidence he had lost being so sick.

"Did Hunter get upset when he found out you were pregnant? Mac would've shot me if I told him I had a baby with The Originals." Gears rubbed the rope back and forth on the wood crate, trying to fray the fibers. The rope loosened a little.

"To say he was less than pleased would be an understatement. When he found out the father was with H.S.P.C., it was even worse." Luna had freed her feet ten minutes ago, and since she'd gotten her hands raised she chewed on the rope. She had tried working on his knots, but the rain had made them bind together.

"I can imagine."

"Hunter assumed that I'd leave as soon as I had Archer. If I left, he'd lose his healer. That's all I really am to him anymore. All our closeness is gone. He took the baby when I stopped nursing and hid Archer from me. I was told that he thought if he kept the baby then I'd never leave. I also heard from some members that he thinks my boy will be the next leader of The Originals."

"Do you want him to be a leader?" Gears heard part of the rope snap and he rolled his shoulders forward slightly. His hands were still bound, but it was an improvement. Blood flooded back into his arms and he winced as some feeling returned.

"I want him to be happy. However, Mother insists he won't be the leader of The Originals no matter what happens." Luna spit out more tiny rope wisps. "Are you okay?"

"I'm just trying to get blood to return to my hands and feet." As soon as Gears spoke, Luna scooted closer to him again and closed her eyes. When she came into contact with his skin, he felt a rush of energy. He felt better instantly. When she opened her eyes to look up at him, he couldn't help himself. He bent down and kissed her lips hungrily. Luna sighed into his mouth. His body reacted. Tied up in the back of a van wasn't the time to be attracted to her, but his body wasn't asking for his permission.

"Why won't you live with me, Luna?" He couldn't help the words from escaping, even though he knew the answer she was going to give him. As he waited for it, he sputtered out a few rope fibers. The kiss was worth having curls of twine clinging to his lips.

"I can't leave Hunter and all those men. I care for them. If there was some other way, or if Hunter and I could make peace, that might be different." Luna set her head on his shoulder and brought her tied hands to her mouth again.

"I don't think I'm enthusiastic about the man who has my child right now," Gears grumbled. Still, he wasn't one to give up. He was going to try to figure out a way to have Luna and his son. He was greedy. He wanted both.

"Hunter does what he thinks is right even if I don't agree. Rumi says 'Out beyond ideas of right-doing and wrong-doing there is a field. I'll meet you there.'"

Gears didn't want to think like that. He wanted to hate the man who was using his child like a pawn to hold Luna. Except logically he knew that wasn't true either. Luna would stay with The Originals with or without her child being here. He understood that. Hunter didn't.

Chen-Ning groaned and the sound blended in with the racket of the van. Gears rocked back and forth and looked under the seat. He could see part of Chen-Ning's face. He looked okay, but he was secured with ropes the same as them. He could imagine how uncomfortable the guard must be.

"I think Chen-Ning isn't injured too badly. Probably waking up with a headache. I wish I could check him for a concussion."

"If I can get close to him when we get out, then I'll help him." Luna leaned against his shoulder and then rolled up onto her knees. She had been doing that on and off for however long they had been in this minivan. When she got to her knees, she popped up just enough to glance out the back window. There was one small corner where the window wasn't taped over with duct tape. Once she glanced out, she quickly dropped back down to the floor. If either of the men saw her, they didn't say anything.

"What do you see now?"

"Huge fancy houses. We're getting close."

Tingling fear began in Gears' stomach. For all the discussion they'd had on the drive, he still didn't have much to trade with Spider. Luna didn't have many suggestions either. He hated to be stuck thinking on the spot. He had to get a plan together. He wished again that he had Mac. Mac could poop out a plan faster than anyone he knew. Sometimes it was a crummy plan, but it'd be something.

A squawk on the radio, followed by garbled talking, could be heard as the vehicle roared along. They decelerated and the van finally came to a halt.

Gears rolled forward. His tied hands struck the bars that held up the bench seat. He was now split apart from Luna. Luna's moonlit hair had dried over the course of the journey and now the lush, thick waves framed her face. How a woman could be so beautiful trussed up in a grubby minivan was beyond him.

Doors slammed. Light blinded him when the back hatch of the minivan rose with a silent swish.

"You guys should get a good mechanic to check your exhaust." Gears blinked into the gray daylight. Rough hands grabbed the front of his shirt, followed by a grunt at his comment. Everything was hard to see through the water spots on his glasses. He squinted as he felt his legs being untied but not his hands.

As he was set on his feet next to the van's bumper, he tried to get his jelly legs to hold him up. Blood rushed back into the appendages. While he swayed, he took in his new surroundings.

Eight men, all armed with a variety of weapons, surrounded him. There were more guns encircling him right now than in Mac's room. Behind him, he felt a pirate holding the ropes at his wrists. Luna was set next to him, then Chen-Ning. In the distance, he could see an intricate metal gate and a brick wall. He knew he was in a completely sealed off compound. He didn't need to be a genius to figure that out.

Chen-Ning was awake but blindfolded and gagged. The young man whipped his head around, probably trying to dislodge the fabric. Three men in oversized fleece coats talked in hushed tones. It gave Gears time to study the area.

They were on an elongated gravel driveway near five lined-up minivans. All along the pebbled half-moon entrance were enormous trees dusted with sparkling snowflakes clinging to the leaves. Men and women dressed in hats and boots were tending lush and exotic plants that had popped above the sprinkle of fresh snow. All over the manicured lawn were sculptures and rock gardens. The place was like a vacation spot, except that this was no vacation that he'd ever want.

The pirates' discussion ended abruptly when a tall, robust Italian male came around the van. Gears and Luna stared at the fat, hairy stranger.

"Vaffanculo, Barker. I told you he wouldn't see you. You lost," the Italian snapped as he glared.

The man who'd yanked Gears out of his car stepped forward.

"I got a trade." Barker pointed at Luna. "This one for my wife."

Gears kept his mouth shut, but there was one thing that wasn't going to happen on this trip. He wasn't going to be separated from Luna. If she ended up stuck in Spider's web, then he was going to be right next to her. Even if they might have to separate at the end of this journey, for now, he was all hers. They were one.

The Italian let his eyes travel briefly over Luna. After her once over, then they went to him. Gears studied the other man back. He guessed him to be in his late forties. The stranger had thick black hair that was slicked back from his forehead and streaked with gray at his temples.

"Come on, Roberto." Barker's huge fist pushed Luna closer, as if the other man had missed her somehow. It wasn't likely. She was beautiful even after being rained on then kept in a van for hours.

Roberto ignored the pirate while his eyes scanned Chen-Ning for a second. Roberto yanked the cloth off of Chen-Ning's eyes, then tugged down the gag. Both pieces of fabric fell around his neck like damp scarves. Chen-Ning's head flipped back and forth.

"I guess we're outnumbered," Chen-Ning whispered.

Luna shushed him.

Gears halfheartedly wished they'd kept him gagged.

"No," Roberto sighed. "No deal."

"I'm not leaving. We're not leaving." Barker spat at the ground. "I want my wife back."

A charged silence descended between the two men. A few of the other pirates around the minivans produced more guns. The action reminded Gears of Karma's secret pockets.

"Fine. You get a five-minute audience." Roberto's brown eyes darkened, then he spun on his heels and strode away. "You owe me, Barker," he called as he vanished past the vehicles.

As soon as the Italian left, Luna was shoved forward. The pirates poked and prodded at them until Gears and Chen-Ning followed the path Roberto had just taken.

On the other side of the van was a sizeable stone opening to a mansion. The stonework and quality was unlike anything Gears had ever encountered before. The three of them, Barker, and two other pirates climbed the gray-and-tan slate steps past marble sculptures of lions.

Even though his glasses were blurred with dried water dots, Gears still noted the massive granite archway as they passed under it. They crossed the threshold past two heavy carved doors and into the Spider's web. When they passed over a sheepskin rug, he was forced to stop, which was good, since halting gave him a minute to adjust his vision to the inside of the house.

They were brought into the marble foyer, his damp sneakers squeaking against the shiny floor. A majestic staircase was the focal point of the room they had entered. His eyes tried to view the paintings on the ceiling, but the art was so high and intricate that after a second he gave up.

At the top of the stairs, on multiple decorative red mats, was a group of people lounging. Some were seated on cushions, some were perched on the railings along the stairs, and others were eating and laughing at low tables. The hum of their conversation hung in the room like the art on the walls. To the right, beyond the main crowd, Gears could hear a group of men arguing. Their voices were raised just above the general din.

Gears was jabbed forward until he was next to Luna at the bottom of the stairs. Chen-Ning was placed on his left so they stood in a line. Negotiation would be what he had at his disposal. What could he provide for this trader? The grandeur of the house didn't give him much hope. This didn't look like a place where money was needed. He could trade medical services, or maybe he could fix something. His eyes jumped to the happily chatting group up on the landing. Not much around here appeared to be broken.

His eyes settled on the staircase and he studied the heavily armed sentries at the top of the landing. Barker stood in front of them with his hands on his hips. Roberto took the stairs three at a time, but when he reached the top, he paused before calling down the hallway. The loud discussion Gears had heard came to an abrupt end. The silence was unsettling, and chills ran down his spine. Some of the women gave them curious glances as the room became hushed.

"Don't mention Spider's age," Luna whispered to him. He wanted to ask why.

"Keep your mouth closed!" Barker snapped at her.

"Spider? Barker would like five minutes of your time," Roberto called down the corridor a second time.

"He can have three," came the sharp response from someone who spoke from the hall out of Gears' line of sight.

The young buck who came to the top of the stairs and looked down at them was wearing a knitted white long-sleeved shirt and extremely tight black pants. His pants were snug enough that Gears wanted to warn him it might not be good for his health. The twenty-something Italian paused on the first stair to push his thick black hair back. Four men flanked him.

Spider had swashbuckling good looks and a hop in his step as he descended the stairs. As he got closer, Gears noted that his left eye was totally green. The iris, pupil, and sclera were all a vibrant green. Around his eye, his eyelashes and eyelid were as black as his wavy hair. The color and blackened skin stood out starkly from his tan completion.

When Spider reached the floor in front of them, his eyes went straight to Barker. The look wasn't friendly.

"What's this?"

"I'll trade you her, for my woman." Barker shoved Luna. She took only one hesitant step to keep herself from falling forward, then straightened to her full height. She was so lovely. Luna looked completely tranquil, like nothing could ever touch her. Gears wasn't fooled. He could see the tight lines around her mouth. He wanted to tell her everything would be okay. He was with her. They were going to be fine—just as soon as he had this figured out. *Think.*

"No." Spider gave her a quick once-over. "No deal." He rubbed his unshaven jaw. Only a bit of black hair had grown on his chin. If he rubbed it too hard it would probably fall off.

The "no" wasn't so bad. If Spider didn't want them, then maybe he could come up with a way to either make a deal with the pirates or escape. There might be more options outside of this mansion.

"She's more beautiful than my wife." Barker reached over and unzipped the front of Luna's sweater. "More pretty than your women. She'd look good here."

Gears' blood simmered. He had to keep his cool. Behind his back, his fingers clenched into a fist. He kept himself from speaking by clenching his teeth together.

"What a douche," Chen-Ning mumbled, shaking his head at Barker. Both Luna and Gears stared at him. Now was not the time for Chen-Ning's continual asinine dialogue.

"Chen, hold your tongue," he hissed. A small part of him wished they would gag him again.

Barker grabbed Chen-Ning by the shoulder and raised his fist, but Spider held up his hand. The pirate let go and stepped back.

Spider's eyes went straight to Chen-Ning. Gears sucked in a breath. Should he say something? For all the times that Chen-Ning spoke when he shouldn't, and for all the times everyone found him annoying, Gears had thought Chen-Ning would be able to spot a moment when he should keep his mouth closed.

"Douche?" Spider asked.

Chen-Ning had been looking at the floor, but now he raised his eyes to Spider.

"Yeah, this guy's a real bait bucket. And this is all kinds of fucked up. I mean, you got a nice place, but then what? You're buying her? What is she, like an ornament?" Chen-Ning shrugged. "That's shitty. You know she's not even that pretty." Chen-Ning rolled his eyes. "Fine. I guess if I *had* to, I'd give her like an eight. That's if I was into women." Chen-Ning's eyes locked on to the other man. "Men are better. How big are you? An eight?" His eyes dropped to Spider's crotch. "We could measure."

Luna shut her eyes then shook her head like she couldn't watch. Gears gaped, utterly shocked. What could Chen-Ning possibly be thinking? He was going to get them shot.

"Who the hell are you?" Spider stepped directly in front of Chen-Ning so they were eye to eye. He crossed his arms over his chest. Two men on the stairs pointed their rifles at Chen-Ning.

"I'm Chen-Ning. You can call me Chen."

"I can call you dog if I want," Spider smiled. He turned away as if to walk back to the stairs, and Gears' shoulders relaxed. Thank God, he wasn't angry. They weren't going to be executed today.

Chen-Ning chuckled. Luna's eyes flew open. They were so close.

"Only if you put a collar on me and take me home." Chen-Ning chuckled again.

Spider spun around, then tipped his head to the side as he eyed Chen-Ning. Chen-Ning wouldn't look down or away. He wouldn't break eye contact. That was too aggressive. Silently, Gears begged Chen-Ning to cower, or at least look contrite.

"Chen, stop talking!" Gears snapped out each word. He was probably making this worse.

"What are you doing here, Chen?" Spider's young, athletic body sauntered toward Chen-Ning and stopped directly in front of him.

"I was trying to help my friends get to Monclova," Chen-Ning answered. Gears saw Luna cringe. Maybe sharing wasn't the best idea.

"You're not doing a very good job." Spider ran his hand down Chen-Ning's arm, his fingers playing with the ropes.

"You're right, I'm not." Chen-Ning grinned then dropped his voice so Spider leaned in. "But I don't mind being tied up, you know, if you're into that."

The two men seemed oblivious that anyone else was around. Gears angled his head to the side as he observed the interaction. Spider offered Chen-Ning a slight smile. Maybe they wouldn't get killed. Chen-Ning and Spider looked like they might have been on a date. Of course, Gears had seen Chen-Ning on a date. Normally it didn't go near as smoothly as this.

"What happened to your eye?" Chen-Ning asked. Luna cringed again. Yeah, this was more like the abysmal Chen-Ning dating that Gears had seen. He shook his head. They were going to get shot after all.

Spider looked like someone had just slapped him. His easy grin vanished and was replaced with a hard-stone frown. His hand went to his belt where a pistol was tucked into the band.

"I was born this way," he snapped as his hand rested on the handgun. "What's it to you?"

"I like it. In Chinese culture, green symbolizes life and peace and…" Chen-Ning paused as his eyes blatantly dropped to the Italian's crotch a second time, "…vitality." Chen-Ning leaned closer to Spider. "So, the name Spider, does that mean you have a web? Can I get caught in it?"

Gears shook his head. What the hell was Chen-Ning doing? Was he hitting on the trader? The guard wasn't even being charming anymore, more like inane.

"Chen," Gears hissed. "Stop it." If they were lucky Spider might think Chen-Ning was just mentally handicapped.

"Barker." Spider suddenly spun away from Chen-Ning. Gears braced for the worst.

"He's only twenty." Gears tried to defend Chen-Ning, but frankly even he didn't know what to say. "He's not the brightest."

"Hey," Chen-Ning harrumphed. "That's uncool, old man."

"Spider, please," Luna begged. "He doesn't mean anything by it."

"Accidenti, Barker." Spider ignored them all and bounded over to the pirate, who was talking to Roberto.

"Yes?" Barker spun around.

"I'll keep them all." The young man waved to Roberto, who was still on the landing. "Get Barker's wife and make sure he leaves." Spider faced Barker. "Next time, don't trade with me unless you're ready to give up the item. I'm not going to play Indian giver with you again. I'll simply kill you and your entire family for the headache."

Barker gave a single solemn nod, then turned to the other men with him. "Move out."

The two sentries on the landing followed the pirates as they went back out the massive front doors. Gears glanced over his shoulder briefly and watched them leave, accompanied with guns aimed at their spines. In hushed tones, Gears could hear Roberto giving orders to one of Spider's men about seeing the pirates escorted off the property with the woman they had come for.

As soon as the hall was empty of the pirates, Spider took a knife from his belt and walked around the three of them. The young man cut Chen-Ning's ropes first. Immediately, Chen-Ning brought his hands to his front and started to rub them together. Gears felt a tugging on his ties next. When his hands were released, he did the same thing as Chen-Ning while Spider freed Luna. Once Luna's hands were no longer bound, Gears reached for her and they linked fingers. Energy and heat filled him. As soon as her palm pressed against him, he felt like someone had just given him a shot of caffeine and B_{12}.

He let go of her for a moment to reach up and take his glasses off. After he cleaned them on his shirt, he perched them back on his nose. The room came into sharper focus.

Spider came around them and stopped directly in front of Chen-Ning again. He sheathed his knife and stared into Chen-Ning's eyes.

"Are you looking for a web to get caught in? If you are, I think you've succeeded."

He nodded.

"If I gotta be stuck in a web, this is a pretty nice one. A hot guy full of vitality isn't so bad, either." He reached up and feathered his fingers around Spider's eye then down his cheek.

Spider cleared his throat. Again, the two men seemed to forget that there were people standing around. Luna was trying not to laugh. Roberto was staring at the ceiling.

"You like my house?" Spider gave only a brief glance to Roberto. "You want a tour?"

"Only if the tour ends in your bedroom," Chen-Ning grinned before he leaned forward and whispered something to Spider that Gears couldn't hear.

"We can start in the bedroom." Spider grabbed Chen-Ning's hand, then climbed the first stair. "Roberto! Put these two somewhere. I don't care where." He started to walk up the stairs with Chen-Ning's hand creeping up the back of his shirt. "I don't want to be disturbed."

"Spider, wait," Roberto called out before Spider reached the landing. "What about Nina? I can't deliver a baby." Roberto took the stairs three at a time and cut off Spider's escape. "And what about Giovanni? He's getting worse."

"What's wrong with Giovanni?" Gears asked, forgetting that he wasn't welcome here. Everyone on the stairs looked to him.

"Gears is a doctor." Chen-Ning leaned on Spider's shoulder and brushed his cheek along the young man's neck. "You can tell him. He's real smart," he murmured. "Brilliant, I'm told."

"H.S.P.C. Gears?" Spider asked. "I've heard of you. I see your gears on the water base towers."

Gears wasn't interested in accolades, if that was where this was going. If someone was sick, he wanted it know.

"Is it Snow Flu?" That was his first concern with them in the house and the number of women he saw around. Snow Flu could spread much too fast. He couldn't let Luna fall ill. He would move Heaven and Earth before he would let that happen.

"Giovanni was shot," Roberto answered. "He won't stop bleeding."

"I can heal and close a wound, but I can't pull a bullet out. Is the bullet still in his body?" Luna asked.

"If you leave the bullet in, doesn't it get infected?" Gears wondered if she had done that before.

"Sometimes it can be alright, but it can cause problems later."

Both of them looked up at Roberto.

"I don't know." Roberto looked to Spider. "You were with him during the fight."

Spider let go of Chen-Ning for a moment and took a few steps down the stairs. He stopped and stared at Luna.

"We have mct, corretta? I knew I recognized you."

Luna nodded.

"Hunter will attack us to get you back," Roberto stated flatly.

Luna nodded again.

"I'll make you both a deal. If you save Giovanni and help Nina with her baby, I'll get you to Monclova."

"We want a full escort. Food and clean clothes as well." Gears glanced at Luna. "Having a baby is messy."

Spider smiled. "We can make a deal."

Chapter 11

"Love is the whole thing. We are only the pieces." Rumi~

"I know you didn't want me to put my hands in there, but the baby was in breech." Gears used his best doctor's voice to subdue a still-irate Roberto. During the birth, he'd discovered that Roberto was a brother-in-law to both Spider and Nina. His family loyalty ran deep, and what he thought was best was not to be questioned. This guy reminded him a little of Mac.

Even though Roberto was still stewing at Gears placing his hands inside Nina, he wasn't letting this become a discussion. He'd done what he had to do for the baby and the mother. He was still shaking from untangling the umbilical cord from around the baby's neck, but he felt better than he had in years. That was probably due to Luna.

"Where is Luna?" He had to see her and make sure she was okay. He'd been with Nina for hours.

Roberto looked to him. He'd been holding Nina's hand and staring at the ceiling while she nursed her new baby. Now he let go and looked at Gears. Gears hid his smile at the slight blush that could be seen creeping under the other man's olive skin.

"She's still with Giovanni." Roberto's eyes dropped to Nina, then popped back up with a slight frown.

"I need to see Luna."

"I'll take you. My sister Donna can look after this." The Italian waved to his sister-in-law and the baby. He looked like he was trying to escape the breast feeding. Swiftly, he opened the door and Gears followed him out. Six women, as well as four men, were standing around in the hallway. He spoke to all of them in quick, clipped

Italian. Gears understood only some of what he said, but apparently, Roberto asked a petite dark-haired woman to look after Nina and her new baby, which she'd decided to name Sofia.

Once they were out into the hall, Gears followed Roberto to a different wing of the massive house. He entered a billiard room with glass cabinets, a bar, and a pool table. Luna leaned over a man who was resting on the center of the billiard table. Her complexion was washed out. Her hair was damp and sticking to her forehead. She didn't look up when they entered.

"My heavens." Gears held himself back from swearing at the sight of her and quickly crossed the thick green carpet between them. "Luna?" He touched her elbow and she jerked for a moment. She was so pale that her face matched her hair. Her blue eyes were lifeless and glazed over.

"Gears?" She ran a tongue over her dry, cracked lips. "I can't stop the bleeding. The metal is in the way, and I can't close around it."

As much as this was about needing an escort to reach Hunter to get his baby, this was also about healing. Healing was in his blood, same as Luna. He eyed the festering wound in the other man's shoulder. The man on the table looked as pale as Luna.

"How much blood has he lost?"

"A lot," she whispered. Gears had to get her to rest. A part of him was demanding he care for Luna as well. "You need to sit."

"I can't let go."

Gears spun around to Roberto. "I want a small knife. I need bandages as well. I would also like your belt."

Roberto hesitated. "A knife? My belt?"

"Luna can't close this. I'm going to have to cut out the bullet. I'll pull the blockage out, then she can work. She can't keep on like this."

"That would help." Luna sagged against his side. "Thank you, my Conpar."

Roberto wavered. "If you kill him, Spider will rip you apart." Roberto handed him a small blade, then started to loosen his buckle.

"I gathered that." Gears grabbed the leather belt and started to make a tourniquet to slow the blood flow.

"I'll go get bandages." Roberto disappeared out the door.

For the next twenty minutes, Gears used the tip of the knife to cut away around the bullet lodged in Giovanni's shoulder. Luna held the belt tight, and it was as if she spoke to the man's body and forced it to bend to her will. Just as he extricated the shell and popped the metal out, Luna began to close the artery. Gears kept the belt tight while she worked, and there was a silent understanding that flowed between them. Luna went to work closing the damaged tissue, and neither of them spoke as she worked. Even though he had seen her gift before, when she closed up the gaping wound where her finger had been cut off, he still watched in awe.

Removing the bullet was much more in his comfort zone than delivering the baby had been. Everything about taking the round out was familiar, and it was nice to have Luna with him. They worked like a team. Seamless. When Roberto returned with bandages, they wrapped the wound and she helped clean up. He didn't even have to ask her for anything. With her, it was as if she could read what his needs were.

When she finally finished, she stood back and gave him a wobbly smile. Instantly, he drew her into his arms.

She sagged against him, and there was no doubt in his mind she was tired. Both the man in him and the doctor in him insisted that she rest.

"Luna needs to sleep."

"Will Giovanni live?" Roberto stood like a silent lookout next to the door.

"He'll live. But he needs rest too. Just let him sleep and have someone keep an eye on him. If he gets a fever, then get me."

Luna nodded, but her eyes were closed. She was falling asleep standing in his arms.

"I got a room you can rest in. I need to update Spider."

Gears agreed. His back was killing him from leaning over the pool table, and he was still trying to catch his breath after delivering the baby.

Following Roberto out into the long hallway, it occurred to him that even though he was tired he felt better than he had in years. His heartbeat was steady and strong. His body felt alive. Luna had saved his life. He held her to him as they were guided to a room at the far end of the hall. Roberto opened the door into a bedroom decorated in blue and gold.

Gears entered and led Luna to the bed. He had her sit under the huge fringed canopy and put her feet up. Roberto paused as Gears looked at one wall that was entirely shelves of jeans. White tags stuck out between the denim.

"I'll check in with Spider. There are clothes in that cabinet and as well as over there." Roberto waved to a closet and then to the sea of jeans. "Don't leave. I'll be back in a little while." He closed the door, leaving them in what Gears would have called the world's largest closet.

"I'm tired," Luna murmured.

Gears wanted to get on the bed with her, but he was covered in blood. She was as well. He spotted a door on the right. Hoping it let into a bathroom, he opened the door and was happy to see a sink, toilet, and small shower.

"I'll get you cleaned up, then you can sleep. Cleanliness is next to godliness."

After grabbing a washcloth and towel, Gears went back to where Luna slumped on the bed. Her eyes fluttered open as he approached.

"How are you feeling?" she asked as he wiped her hands and arms clean.

"Me?" Gears chuckled. "Don't worry about me. You, on the other hand, look awful, like warmed over death."

"Telling someone they look bad isn't a nice thing to say." Luna gave a pout, then sat up slowly.

"That's what I said to Chen," he laughed. He was going to tell her to just stay still, but then her hands gripped the bottom of her shirt. She yanked the garment off then tossed it to the floor.

"If you're feeling fine, I could use some energy."

"What?"

Luna shimmed out of her skirt. She then kicked off her tennis shoes. They bounced next to the foot of the bed. Her socks went next.

"You could energize me." Her fingers went to the zipper of his jeans. She unbuttoned his pants, and once they were loose she slipped them down.

"What?" His eyes were on the little nest of curls at the junction of her legs.

She smiled.

Gears grinned. "I only say 'what' when I'm with you." He paused. "I don't know, Luna."

"I know." Luna unhooked her bra and the cups fell to the bed beside her. "Connecting to you would make me feel like myself again."

Gears looked behind him at the door.

"Roberto might be back any moment. We're in the house of some kind of trader, and we're looking for our son." Gears pushed his glasses up his nose. "I guess this is me getting involved." He cupped her breast. "Chen-Ning would be proud."

Luna laughed as they reached for his shirt together.

Chapter 12

"Be drunk in love. Since love is everything that exists." Rumi~

The knock on the door woke him from his sexual slumber. He reached for Luna but felt empty pillows. His eyes popped open. Luna wasn't in the room with him. The knock came again.

Gears grabbed his jeans, which were stiff with blood, and tugged them on. He got up, opened the door and peeked out.

Roberto stood in the hallway.

"Ciao, Gears." Roberto raised an eyebrow. "Spider wants to speak to you. Luna is already in the dining room. You're expected to join her."

Gears nodded. He glanced down at his pants.

"Use whatever clothes you would like. Spider says he would like you to join him for dinner."

Dinner. Was it evening already? Gears had completely lost track of time.

"One minute." He nodded again to Roberto.

"You can have more than a minute." Roberto looked down at his jeans and then to his hair. "If you would like to shower that's fine. I'll wait."

Gears gave another quick nod then hurried to the bathroom. He washed quickly, toweled himself dry, then returned to the blue bedroom scanning for clothes. A blue button-up shirt caught his eye. The top was on a chair with a pair of black jeans folded next to it. Luna must have picked them out.

Since he didn't want to keep Spider waiting, he picked up the garments and dressed. He decided he looked presentable enough to face whatever was next.

Opening the door, he then followed Roberto down the grand staircase. When they reached the dining area, Gears found the room as impressive as the rest of the house. A long gleaming mahogany table sat in the center of a massive hall filled with plants, art, and flickering wall sconces.

As he crossed under a chandelier, he noted that men and women took up both sides of the table with food platters spread out between them. The smell of breads, meats, and spices filled the air around him. There was a mix of joyful chatter as he entered. Soft music drifted in.

Spider sat at the head of the table on what appeared to be a loveseat overflowing with a dozen blankets and pillows. Chen-Ning was wrapped around the trader like a shawl. Chen-Ning's head rested on Spider's shoulder, and his hands were low enough on his stomach that Gears had the feeling they were trying to go lower. Gears took only a handful of steps toward Spider before he spotted Luna.

Luna had been seated to the right of Spider, in a wooden chair like all the other occupants in the room. She stood when she saw him and came around the table to greet him. Gears forgot to walk when he saw her. Luna was radiant. Her glow had returned and her skin looked healthy and clear. Her waist-length hair circled lovingly around her, and she wore blue jeans and a pale pink top that molded to her breasts. Gears stared as he remembered his mouth sucking on those breasts a few hours ago.

"Doctor Gears." Spider's voice carried over the crowd, and his name pulled him out of the trance Luna had sucked him into. Her eyes danced a bright blue when she reached for his hand. With his palm securely fastened to hers, he walked over to stand in front of Spider.

The men and women continued to talk, but the conversation became hushed as he got closer to Spider. Gears had the feeling they were waiting to see what would happen. When Gears reached Spider's side, a man got up and offered his chair to him. Obediently, he sat. Luna sank into a chair next to him.

"A toast." Spider waved, and a pretty girl with a tray presented two shot glasses filled to the brim with a clear liquid. She set one tiny glass in front of Gears and the other in front of Spider. The room became silent.

Spider leaned forward in his chair and Chen-Ning leaned back. It was the first time that Gears had seen the two men separate even a little bit since they met.

"To Nina and her little one, Sofia." Spider raised the glass, tipped his head back then drank the shot.

Everyone stared at Gears, and Luna nodded to the glass. "No, thank you" wasn't an option.

Gears followed suit while the words "salute" and "cheers" were called out from around the table. The alcohol burned all the way down, and he coughed. He wasn't much of a drinker, but he didn't think this would be the time to say that. He licked his lips.

"A toast." Spider waved his hand to the girl with the tray again. "To Giovanni." The shot glasses were refilled. Gears sighed. Since dealing with his heart condition was always his concern he had stayed away from drugs and liquor, but as he glanced around, he knew without a doubt it would be an insult not to drink. "No" was still not an option.

"Evviva!" Spider raised his glass and drank. Gears did as well. Luna pressed her palm to his.

"And now." Spider had the shots filled again. "A toast to my Chen. Who is staying here with me."

Gears eyes went from the drinks to Chen-Ning.

"That wasn't part of the deal." Gears sprang to his feet. To say nothing and leave Chen-Ning here just to save his own skin wasn't right. He couldn't stay silent.

Spider stood up.

"I'm changing the deal."

"I'm not going to leave Chen-Ning." Behind him, he heard someone pull out a weapon and the familiar click of a safety being switched to semi.

"Hey, old man." Chen-Ning slipped from behind Spider and put his hand on his lover's chest. "Gino, let me talk to Gears."

Spider took the shot, slapped the glass to the table, then sat. He kept glaring.

"Gears." Chen-Ning faced him. "I'm going to stay. I'm not asking your permission."

"He'll dump you. I don't want to say it, but I know your track record. Once he's done with you, then what?"

Chen-Ning grinned. "I can't explain this to a man all boring and logical like you, but I'm going to try. Can you understand that I love him? I'm going to stay. I'll die without him. He's worth the risk. Drink to my happiness and go on to Monclova."

This was ludicrous. The problem was, he *did* understand. At the end of this journey, he would never want to leave Luna. Gears felt like a part to him would die when she wasn't with him. It wasn't the part that kept his heart beating or his brain working; it was the part that made life livable, enjoyable, and worth everything including the risks.

"Does he know who you are?" Gears pushed up his glasses.

"Yeah, Gino knows I'm H.S.P.C. and that I was a water base guard. He knows all that. He still wants me, and…" Chen-Ning dropped his voice, "…Italian men are the way to go."

"What happens when he doesn't want you anymore?"

"Still an eighty-year-old man," Chen-Ning chuckled. "You know you're not my father, right?"

"I can still worry no matter how old I am."

Spider stood again and wrapped an arm around Chen-Ning's waist.

"I will never be without Chen. He makes me laugh. He stays, and I'll kill anyone who would try to change that." Spider sat again with his hand still lingering on Chen's thigh.

"That's sweet, Gino." Chen-Ning turned around and climbed back onto the other man's lap. "You love me enough to kill people. That's the dream."

Spider laughed.

From across the table, Roberto nodded to Gears. A silent sign, perhaps, that Spider was going to be true to his word.

"A drink to my new home with Gino." Chen-Ning reached over and pushed the shot glass toward Gears.

Gears conceded. He couldn't control Spider or Chen-Ning. All he really could do was hope for the best. He lifted the shot and took a deep breath, preparing for the burn. He drank quickly and tried to cover his cough. For all the things he was good at, it appeared consuming large quantities of alcohol wasn't one of them.

Spider stood and smiled.

"And now a drink to Luna and Gears, who will be on their way tomorrow morning. My best vehicles and men will escort you."

Gears sighed and then hiccupped. He looked at the shot glass, which seemed to have refilled itself by magic. Well, he *had* to drink to leaving. This was what he wanted. On to Mexico to see his baby. He smiled as he lifted the shot. He was excited to meet his child, but the excitement was at war with the thought of being parted from his Luna.

He held up the drink. The room blurred and he pushed up his glasses. They drank the shot together.

"Now we eat!" Spider called out.

Food was passed around. Luna fed him spicy meats and rich sauces that he normally would have avoided. Gears licked her fingers clean. Music played more loudly from somewhere, and his head became fuzzy. Lights twinkled. The laughter and Luna's touch made him forget she might be away from him come tomorrow. Gears was dragged out of his chair when Luna wanted to dance.

Powerless to fight her, he spun around and drank shots until he lost count. The night seemed to swallow him up as he toasted a final glass with Chen-Ning, bidding his friend a sad farewell.

As the night headed toward early morning, Luna and he talked of his life on the water base. He had no sense of time other than he felt the minutes leading up to Luna taking him back to their bedroom weren't passing quickly enough.

"My match," Luna whispered as she helped him up to their room. "Make love to me once more."

Gears nodded. Yes. He would hold her before time ran out. The room spun. First, he would sleep for just a moment.

Chapter 13

"I am yours. Don't give myself back to me."

Rumi~

The hangover was colossal. Even though he knew it was just severe dehydration, the knowledge didn't help the pounding at his temples. Gears slept in the back of an armored limousine that he had been told to get into in the early morning. Other than Chen-Ning giving him a pistol and wishing him safe travels, the early hours were a blur.

Luna's hand was in his hair, sliding some of the tendrils back. He leaned up and looked at her.

"Are you feeling better?" she asked him as he sat up. Better? Well, he didn't want to vomit anymore. If that was better than he supposed he should say yes. He reached for a bottle of water in a cup holder and chugged it. Then he looked around the inside of the car. "You look like death warmed over," she giggled.

"Death warmed over? More like I'm leftover death microwaved a few times then left cold on the counter." This morning when he had gotten into the vehicle, there had been two other men with Luna and him. He'd fallen asleep while trying not to puke, but now as he glanced around the posh black leather interior he realized the men were gone and they were all alone.

"That bad?"

"I'm okay." He noticed the divider between the front and the back was closed off as well. "Where is everyone?"

"They got out." Luna shrugged. "I asked them to let us be alone a few miles back. One of the guys is riding in the front with the driver and the other man is in one of the Jeeps behind us."

"Why?" Gears asked as he looked out the back window. He could see the rest of the convoy in a line. He counted four vehicles, two Jeeps and two trucks.

"Because ahead of us is uncertainty, and to continue this leg of our journey I thought you might need to feel a little better."

"What?"

"We talked about this last night." A smile tugged on Luna's lips. He should thank her for not pointing out that he had asked "what" again.

Gears set his head on her shoulder and took a deep breath. Last night was a haze. They'd had sex, he thought. The evening was a wild and crazy haziness, unlike anything he'd ever done before. They drank, ate, and danced. Talking didn't come to him. If they had spoken about something, he only remembered tiny snippets like her charming laughter and his whispers that he loved her.

"Last night was…" Gears paused. He didn't want to lie. "We made love, and was I…" He paused again. "Did I do something wrong? Was it satisfying?"

Luna giggled "We didn't have sex. We talked." Luna stroked her fingers through his hair. "I know you don't feel well. I asked the men for us to be alone because I thought I could share some of my energy with you. We could make up for what we didn't do last night."

Gears was catching on. She wanted to have sex with him in the limo. He should be pardoned for his slow uptake, since it felt like his head might fall off.

"No way." He lifted his head then glanced out the window like someone could be watching him right now. Outside was only a barren landscape with broken houses, rusted cars, and struggling foliage.

"I just know I'm going to miss you. This is our last chance." Luna sat looking out the window as silence descended between them. He didn't like that he had no idea what she was thinking.

He sighed.

"Luna, I care about you, and it seems wrong to have sex with you like this."

"Like what?"

"In the back of a car right before we are going to find our son and face The Originals." Gears leaned forward on the seat and sipped more water. "I'm not the kind of wild guy that would have intercourse with a woman in a moving car. Around you, I'm trying to be a good man, Luna. I want to be good for you."

"You're right. Around me you're not a good man." Luna wouldn't look at him. "I think you're not just good, you're brilliant."

Every time she said that, it made him smile. Luna loved him in her own special way, and sometimes that included having sex while she was a prisoner in an interrogation room, or after she'd cut off her finger, or in the world's biggest closet.

He drank the rest of his second bottle of water while he thought about her request. He did want her. There never seemed to be a time he could shut off his desire for her. His cock stirred. His mind thought sex was a bad idea, but the rest of him was on board.

"At the end of this trip, I don't know when I'll be able to connect with you again. We talked about this last night." Luna's eyes caught his. She turned in her seat, then licked her lips. "This is it, my match."

"Goodbye?" He felt like she was driving a knife into the heart she had fixed.

"Rumi says," Luna gave him a sad smile, "'goodbyes are only for those who love with their eyes. Because for those who love with their heart and soul, there is no separation.'"

Tears formed in her eyes and he wanted them gone. He yanked her into his arms. She pressed her face to the crook of his neck, and his hangover abated with just that little bit of contact. Her mouth pressed to his neck as she rained kisses along his collarbone. He was going to give in. If she wanted him right now, he would strip naked for her in the back of a moving car.

Luna worked her way up to his mouth. "Gears," she whispered. His name was a breathy moan on her lips. Her water-blue eyes smoldered as he slid his hand into her hair, twisting the strands and pulling her mouth closer. Their lips met. Heat exploded between them like a lightning arc. She bit down on his lip, and desperation born of the fear of losing her blossomed inside of him. He opened his mouth. Their tongues intertwined. Her scent was more intoxicating than the alcohol he had consumed the night before. He could never fight her, and if he was honest with himself he didn't want to resist.

This was probably a bad idea. He normally thought things through, but that wasn't going to happen just now. A shudder ripped through his body at the feel of her soft curves against him. He jerked his mouth away and encircled her with his arm. He tightened his hand around her waist as he slipped off the leather seat to kneel in front of her.

"Do you remember what you told me last night?" Luna panted. She toed off her shoes and undid the top of her jeans.

"No." While leaning back, he tugged out of his shirt and undid the button of his pants as well. He licked his lips as she yanked off her socks and slipped off the seat to the floor ahead of him.

"You said you always wanted to try something." Luna grabbed the bottom of her shirt and pulled it over her head.

Gears was in the process of pulling down his zipper when his hand stopped. Oh, Good Lord, no! He had told her his secret. He wished he could close his eyes and erase whatever happened last night. *I'm never going to drink again*, he told God.

"Please tell me that I didn't say…" He couldn't say it out loud, at least not when he was sober. How drunk was he last night? "I lied," he said quickly.

"No, you didn't." Luna shimmed out of her jeans and turned around on her knees. She bent over slightly on the seat. His mouth went dry. Her position was so hot it had his cock pulsating. If he didn't get control of himself soon he would come in his pants. No one other than Luna had ever had the ability to make him this horny this fast.

Luna looked over her shoulder at him. His eyes gazed at her smooth, rounded ass. It was as perfect as the rest of her. He held in a groan.

"Don't hold back," she murmured.

"Luna, I think—" Gears braced her hands on either side of the seat. Once her fingers were dug into the soft leather, he ran his palms up and over her arms. Her skin was so soft it felt like silk.

"Stop thinking. For a moment, don't be Gears, a brilliant doctor, be Adam, a man, my match."

He dropped a kiss to her shoulder, then rained more down over her back, pushing her hair aside as he went. A whimper escaped her. Yes, right now he just wanted to be the man who loved her. She arched her back into him, brushing her ass against his jeans and the throbbing member still encased inside of the fabric.

Gears could smell the unique scent of her as she spread her legs wider for him. He positioned himself between her legs as her wet scent taunted him. He sucked in a deep breath, promising himself he would never forget a moment of being with her until the day he died. He tried to find some calm, but with her bent over like this it was too erotic for calm. He felt excited, and all hers.

He pulled his zipper all the way down, then shoved at his jeans until they fell around his knees. He leaned his weight on his hands on both sides of her waist. He buried his nose in her hair while his fingers brushed along the smooth skin of her ass cheeks. His cock was now free of its fabric prison, and it eagerly bounced toward her. His control was slipping. He tried to clear his head, but Luna's ass kept dancing in his mind.

She pushed back against him, and the soft curve of her ass rubbed against his hard cock.

"I'm not going to do it." He put his hand at her lower spine to still her swaying hips. "It's just something I've thought about, that's all."

"No more thinking."

But he needed to think. He needed his sanity to return. Was he really considering having anal sex in the back of a car? He didn't do things like that. Gears wasn't an uncivilized sex fiend.

The interrogation room popped into his head. Maybe he was a tad uncivilized. He moved both hands so his fingers could trail down the back of her arms again. Luna gasped when he slipped his hands around her body to grip her breasts then tease her nipples. Her breasts were like warm satin. The weight felt incredible in his palms. The sex on his bed the first time he met her danced in his head. Yeah, he was a sex fiend. He loved all her perfect curves. He loved her. He wanted her. Maybe she was right and thoughts had no place here between them.

Luna was his. The heat of her skin saturated his palms, and her nipples jutted against his hands. He flicked his nails over the hard tips and she gasped, then wiggled again.

Slipping one hand down her belly, he reached her underwear. They were pale pink, with lace. He didn't know where she'd gotten them, but he silently thanked whoever had given them to her. He hooked his finger in the fabric and pulled them to the side. Desperation fisted in his stomach. He had the urge to take her hard and fast. Just like the first time, there was something primal in him that was taking over. Taking his cock in his hand, he rubbed the head against her slick lips.

"Don't fight it. Do what you want to do," Luna urged. "I'm with you." Her hips moved and swayed, letting him become wetter with her juices. Need, stronger than he had ever known, gripped his mind. His cock moved up to the tight entrance. He spread more of her wetness over the puckered hole.

"I want you here." His voice didn't even sound like his any longer. "I can't think anymore." He brought his fingers to her ass and pressed against the hole. She sighed, then shivered, but she didn't pull away or try to stop him. His head spun, and it wasn't because of the night of drinking any more.

Gears worked his fingers back and forth over her anus, then slowly sank one finger inside. She moaned, and he added a second finger. He began to stroke her chute, widening her with each thrust. The muscles of her ass gripped him tight, but she pressed back into him, giving him more access. The heat of her pulsated around him. He took his cock into his hand and ran the head of around the tight hole. More of his pre-cum beaded and gathered. He couldn't wait any longer.

Sliding the head of his cock into her ass, he paused and dipped his fingers into the sweet cream of her slit. He glided the wetness over his dick, then pressed forward a little more. They both groaned. She felt so tight, so incredible. He thrust deeper still. The angle against the seat in the car was almost painful, but he didn't care. He wasn't stopping. She shoved back against him, rocking her hips to make small, shallow thrusts. They began to move together as he adjusted himself and she leaned back. His lower belly began to slap against her backside. The sound was loud in the confines of the car. His breath bellowed out, making her hair flutter over her shoulders. The fingers that were still holding her panties out of the way slid around to press hard on her clit. Each thrust rubbed his thumb on her flesh, and she gasped with every stroke.

"It's so damn good." The words were out of his mouth before he even realized he'd sworn.

"Yes."

The feel of her wetness on his fingers made him hotter. Her ass was gripping perfectly around his cock again and again. He clenched his teeth. He was so close to exploding inside of her. He tried to close his eyes and review some medical documents to gain part of his sanity. He refused to climax before she did. He rolled his fingers over her little nub. Luna's back bowed. He could feel her muscles begin to contract. Her ass was getting tighter, if that was possible.

She moaned as her head fell forward onto the leather seat. He bent forward all the way to her back, then opened his mouth over her ear. He sucked and nipped lightly at the shell. Animal cries surrounded him. Were they hers or his? He could feel the moisture increase.

"Yes, Gears. Yes." Luna panted.

Gears listened to her moan as he slammed his cock deep, driving his hips forward in short, rough thrusts. A sob was torn from her, followed by a sharp cry. She rocked back onto him, shuddering.

All his. He moved his hand to her hips and gripped her thighs with his fingers digging into the soft flesh. He let his control go. He hammered his length into her back sheath. For one heartbeat, then two, his body convulsed then he jetted his seed inside of her. His heart was pounding. Fire was flowing through his veins. He slumped forward, burying his face into the back of her neck.

So many different emotions flooded his system all at once. Sadness was trying to take over. He didn't want to leave her. Second came sedated and happy. Third... he was embarrassed. Anal sex wasn't like him, but he wouldn't have traded the experience for the world. Last, fear for her plagued him. He loved her. Gears loved her like he would never love anyone else, ever. Her sayings, her kindness, her pushing him to let go and just feel things. All of that made Luna, and it was perfect. How would he ever let her go?

Gears slipped gingerly out of her backside then sank to the floor of the car. He rolled to his side as Luna dropped off the seat to sit next to him. He helped her arrange her underwear and pull her pants back on, but his hands were still shaking. After they were both semi-dressed, he hugged her to him.

"I have RCC100 in my backpack. Roberto got my bag from the pirates before they left. I would like to…" Gears paused. He was a doctor, for Pete's sake. Normally, talking about this kind of human anatomy wasn't hard for him. "I'd like to put my special cream where I…"

"I can heal myself," Luna giggled. "But thank you, Romeo. I don't need any more of your special cream right now."

Gears smiled as a past conversation with Mac popped into his head. Now he understood why his friend wanted him to stop calling RCC100 that. Gears smiled as he let the car rock them. His eyes drifted shut while he held her. He would recline on the floor of the limousine with Luna for just a few minutes more. When he got up and finished getting dressed, then he would think about their future.

"Luna?" he murmured. Odd, but his hangover was gone. She had healed him again.

"Yes?"

"Before I leave with Archer, promise me that you'll think about coming home with me. Just think about it. I love you." He couldn't contain the words. He would never not love her. She was his.

"I'll think about it." Luna pushed up his glasses. "But please do something for me. Remember this Rumi quote whenever we're not together."

"What is it?"

"'Close your eyes. Fall in love. Stay there.'" She settled against his chest as they sped toward his baby.

Chapter 14

*"Love rests on foundation. It is an endless ocean,
with no beginning or end." Rumi~*

Luna directed the convoy to stop at the edge of the city. She got out of the car and pulled on a long green coat. Gears got out of the car behind her as he tugged on a leather jacket.

"This is where we need to be dropped," Luna said as Roberto got out of the vehicle ahead of their car.

"Here?" Gears pulled his backpack on. Before them was a city of tin huts and broken-down cars and trucks.

Along the road there had only been a smattering of dwellings, but up ahead there were seas of houses. Where were they going to find Archer?

Roberto must have thought the same thing. He got out then looked from Luna to the city of Monclova.

"Are you sure you want us to leave you here?"

"Yes," Luna nodded. "I was told that Hunter is in a house a few blocks from here. The people around his house are mostly Original members. It's safer if we leave you here and Gears and I walk. I don't want a shootout where I have to fix more bullet holes."

Roberto nodded. "Fair enough." He called to the rest of the men. "Andiamo."

The cars pulled away just as Luna darted between a large chain-link fence and a handful of overgrown weeds. Gears didn't get a chance to see their protection disappear. He had to chase after Luna's jogging form. They weaved between two close-together houses then slipped past a tin can that he thought no one should live in. Finally, he caught up with Luna and grabbed her arm. She paused, then tugged him down next to a round trash bin overflowing with plastic bottles.

"Why are you running?" he asked as he caught his breath. He might have felt better than he had in years, but jogging wasn't something he had done enough of to avoid being winded.

"Word will spread that Spider was here. The Originals will be on the lookout. The idea is that we get in while they are all out trying to figure out what Spider is doing. That car we came in will make a diversion for us." Luna stood then moved around the trash receptacles.

Gears got up and followed her. "Have you been here before?"

"No. Hunter has been moving from place to place to hide from me, but I've got friends who keep me in the know. Now that you're here, we can get Archer and make sure he's safe. Are you worried?"

"No." Surprisingly, he wasn't. The only thing he was concerned about was losing her when his baby was in his arms. He slipped past a burned-out Buick and had to pick up his speed again to keep up with her graceful lope.

"When we get there," Luna glanced behind her and her bright blue eyes flashed, "I'll stand watch. You grab Archer. Once we have him, I've got a friend on the other side of Monclova who owes me for saving his life. We go there next."

"He'll get us out?"

"He'll get a car that you can take back to Headquarters. Hopefully, the ride back will be smoother than the trip here."

Gears was about to agree, but when he thought about it, he decided he wouldn't have traded any of his time with Luna. Even if he had been shot at, his car went off the road, and tied up by pirates, every second he had with Luna was worth it.

Luna halted suddenly and pressed herself flat against a blackened metal shed. He did the same thing as two men walked by.

"It's that one there." Luna pointed to a boarded-up house squished next to a limp garage. All the windows had wood and nails covering them. A red spray-painted circle around the letters H.S.P.C. marked the dwelling.

"Hunter is in there?"

"No." She shook her head. "We passed Hunter a while ago. I saw him talking to someone when we were next to the trash." Luna pointed at the house. "Archer is in there. I know it."

Gears nodded and stepped toward the house. He didn't make it past the end of the building before Luna grabbed his hand. She pulled him close and pressed her lips to his. Her tongue slipped into his mouth, and he kissed her back, pressing her to him.

When he lifted his head, her eyes were damp with tears.

"Luna, what is it?"

"Promise me that no matter what, you'll take Archer and protect him. I want you both safe. You both matter to me."

"You matter to me," Gears sighed. "What about you being safe?"

"Things are not easy for Romeo and Juliet," she whispered. "Promise me my son will be with you."

"I'll get Archer." He wasn't going to promise much else. He was still not giving up on the idea that he could have a future with Luna.

As soon as the street was deserted, Gears let go of her hand and they crossed. Luna might have been right. It seemed like everyone had vanished. If they were all off wondering what Spider was doing in town, then he might be able to get in and get out without problems. They crossed the street then slipped up to the house. He prayed all the while he picked the lock on the front door. When the door opened, he said a silent thank you to Karma, who had taught him the skill of lock-picking the same day he taught her how to use his label maker.

The inside of the house was nicer than the outside. Upon entering, Gears scanned the living room. He crossed over the stained carpet and past two couches that faced each other with a rug between them. On his right was a hallway, and straight ahead opened up into a small kitchen area.

"Archer is down the hall in the bedroom. I'm going to grab a few things we'll need and keep an eye out."

Gears nodded to Luna then hurried down the dimly lit hallway. As he walked, he opened up doors. First a bathroom, then a room filled with boxes and containers.

As he entered the last door, he spotted a bed in his direct line of sight, and then, to his right, a low crib. The moment seemed big, but he didn't have the luxury of taking it all in. Instead, he rushed to the plastic spindles and looked down. Sleeping peacefully was the most beautiful baby he had ever seen.

There might be handsomer babies in this world, but at this moment, Gears was sure he had the most amazing child ever created.

Reaching down, he lifted the boy into his arms. They had made it. He had his baby. With tears gathering in his eyes, he pressed his face to the boy's soft cheek.

"Gears!" Luna's frantic call yanked him out of the moment with his baby boy.

Gears rushed out of the bedroom then hurried to the living room. When he spun around the corner, he stopped dead in his tracks.

Luna was face down on the floor with a man standing over her. The huge brunet had his foot on the center of Luna's back. Gears had no doubts that this must be Hunter.

Hunter's burly frame filled the center of the room. He looked like he was easily three hundred pounds of pure muscle. It struck Gears that he was handsome. The only thing that detracted from his striking good looks was a scar that ran from his cheek down his neck.

Hunter's large black boot ground down into Luna's spine. She threw her hand behind her back, trying to strike at his leg, but her flailing made no difference in his position. The gun that Chen-Ning had given him felt real and solid where it was tucked into the waistband of his pants along his spine. Gears was a pacifist, but he wasn't going to let Hunter hurt Luna. He would kill him first.

"Give me Archer." Hunter gave the soft command as he pulled a pistol from a holster on his belt. He aimed at Luna's head. "Give the baby to me. Now!"

Outside the house, Gears saw a shadow pass the wood slats. Someone was yelling in the distance. A woman was screaming. All around this private standoff chaos was erupting. Hunter noticed the commotion as well. He glanced to the front window next to the door of the house, where there was a small gap in the planks. It was mostly boarded up, so Gears wondered if he might have a better view through the wood laths than he did.

"Don't do it," Luna's muffled voice came from the floor. "You promised you would take him to the H.S.P.C."

"Shut it, Luna," Hunter barked. "H.S.P.C. is the last place Archer's going."

"He won't kill me." Luna sounded a little calmer than before. "Just leave with Archer."

"Fuck the H.S.P.C." Hunter brought his gun from pointing at Luna to aiming at Gears and the baby. "Archer isn't leaving, and neither is Luna."

Tucking Archer, who still slept soundly, closer to his body, Gears reached behind him. Hunter's eyes were on Gears adjusting the baby. With a quick sweep of his hand, Gears snatched the handgrip of the gun and jerked it out from his pants.

Gears held his pistol out and faced Hunter.

Hunter laughed. "Your hands are shaking."

"Let her go." Yes, his hands might not be so steady, but his voice was.

Hunter lifted his boot from Luna's back. She stood unsteadily. Her face was red and tears streaked down her cheeks. As soon as she rose, Hunter's hand snaked out and caught her by the neck. His giant hand wrapped all the way around the fragile column. Luna's hand grabbed at his, her fingers tugging ineffectually.

"Give me Archer and I'll let you go."

"Gears, please. He won't shoot Archer. Use the baby as a shield and leave. Spider's men are still here. I think they're attacking."

"Shut it, Luna," Hunter repeated.

Struggling for air and coughing, she tried to tug on Hunter's arms again.

"No, Hunter. The baby is his." She hit at his hand. Outside, Gears could hear more yelling and another scream. "Spider's men are raiding." Luna's nails dug into Hunter's wrist. "You can get out of here."

"I swear, Luna, one day I'm going to kill you." Hunter's forearm flexed. Her face turned from red to purple.

"Let her go." Gears' finger smoothed along the trigger. He wanted to shoot, but he wasn't a hundred percent sure he wouldn't hit Luna. All those times Mac had told him to practice shooting, he had ignored him. He was kicking himself now. He glanced down at Archer. The baby still slept.

"Leave," she wheezed. Her eyes turned to the man strangling her. "Let him go, Hunter, and I'll stay with you until the day you die."

Gears needed a plan. Luna couldn't stay here. How was he going to get out of this mess?

The last of her words got Hunter to release her neck. She fell face down on the floor and coughed as she tried to take in some much-needed oxygen.

Hunter's glare went from Gears' face to Luna. Hunter was clearly not concerned that Gears was still pointing a gun at him. He crouched next to Luna.

"You'll give me your word, Luna. If I let this H.S.P.C. trash leave, you'll stay. You aren't leaving ever again."

Gears sucked in a deep breath.

"No. Don't agree to that." He couldn't stop himself from cutting in. He had to think. He needed a plan. Mac was the only person on this Earth who would be able to come up with a way to fix this off the cuff. Gears was smart, but he didn't have a head for negotiations that involved guns. "She isn't staying."

Hunter stood slowly from where he'd crouched. His blue eyes were like ice chips.

"This doesn't concern you anymore." Hunter smiled at Luna. "Tell your little friend that you're staying, Luna. Do it and I'll let him live." Hunter raised his gun and again aimed the barrel exactly at Gears' heart. "Two in the head and one in the heart. Then I'm going to hold you down and make you watch him die. You won't be able to save him." Hunter nudged her with his boot.

Luna rose onto her knees. She brushed away the tears and gave him a small smile.

"Romeo and Juliet didn't end up together either," she whispered.

"We aren't Romeo and Juliet," Gears snapped.

"You're right." Luna shook her head sadly. "We are going to live at the end of our story." She glanced up at Hunter. "If you let Gears and Archer live, and if you let them leave here, I promise to stay here with you. I won't ever leave you again."

Hunter slipped his gun back into his holster. He took two huge steps toward Gears, and before Gears could do anything, Hunter swiped the gun out of his hand like the weapon was a toy.

"You didn't even take the safety off," Hunter laughed at him. Then his expression became serious. "Let me see my nephew."

The word "nephew" shocked Gears. He was so stunned that he didn't move when Hunter took Archer from his arms.

Like a magical spell, Hunter's eyes softened. He held the baby and whispered a soft goodbye before kissing the baby's cheek.

"If Spider is attacking us, you won't get out of here alive, and you might kill Archer during your escape." Hunter rocked the baby back and forth. "Whatever deal Luna just made for your sorry hide isn't going to help you once you leave this house."

Gears pushed up his glasses, then accepted the child back into his embrace. Hunter was most likely right. He looked to Luna still kneeling on the floor. This wasn't right. He was leaving here without her, and he didn't even know how he was going to get out of Monclova keeping Archer safe.

"Spider has no allegiance to anyone," Hunter smirked. "Not a good choice in friends for—"

The first bullet hit the door. Hunter was cut off midsentence. He immediately tackled Gears to the floor. He didn't pay much attention to Gears specifically, but he seemed to be throwing himself over the baby. Luna threw herself flat to the carpet again. Gears found himself squished under the huge man. More bullets hit the entrance and the window. What was left of the glass shattered.

Outside the screaming and yelling got louder. Men called to each other. Gears cuddled around the baby but at the same time tried to wiggle free to protect Luna. More rounds hit the wall behind him as Luna wiggled across the floor toward him. Her hand reached out for his, and they linked fingers as another piece of glass from the window fell.

"You and Archer have to get out of here!" Luna called to him above what he thought might be a semiautomatic.

"We all have to get out of here." He turned to Hunter. "You're helping us."

"I've lived here only a few days; do you think I know something I'm not telling you?" Hunter checked his clip and handed Gears' pistol back to him. "We're pinned down."

The wood door to the house was barely hanging on the hinges. He looked first to the exit, then to the hall.

"We have to get to the back bedroom and climb out the window." Gears tucked Archer to his left side and gripped his pistol tightly.

"We might be surrounded," Hunter argued.

"Better to check then to just stay trapped here." Gears inclined his head at Luna and she scooted closer to him. "Unless you have a better idea."

Hunter nodded. Then, for a heartbeat, the bullets stopped. Were they reloading? As the brief silence enclosed around them, Hunter took Archer and handed the baby to Luna. She snuggled him to her side. The boy still slept. He was shocked the violence hadn't awakened his child.

Gears was still marveling at the baby's ability to sleep through gunfire when a thunder of sound ripped through the room.

The door to the house was kicked in. Wood, the hinges, and the knob all scattered across the room. Gears threw his hands over Luna to shield her from the flying splinters as best he could.

When he glanced up, the shadow of a man filled the doorway. Red hair flamed like a beacon.

Chapter 15

"There is a subtle truth: whatever you love you are." Rumi~

Mac stepped into the room with two weapons at the ready. A rifle was slung on his back and he was in full armor. That armor Gears had created for him. Gears heard a slight rustle of sound behind him. When he glanced to the hall, Karma was crouched like a sleek black cat in the shadow of the doorway. She was also armed with two modified pistols. He had worked on those weapons as well.

She didn't give him her normal soft smile when their eyes met. She looked pissed. Actually, they both did.

For a second, Gears wasn't sure if he was safest with Hunter or Mac. His friend was going to kill him for leaving, and for scaring the bejesus out of him. Gears decided after a second that Mac was the man he should pick. Before he let go of Luna to rise, Mac's greeting made him pause.

"The interrogation room has cameras," Mac's voice rumbled. Gears wished a hole would open up and he could disappear. Embarrassment painted his face.

He let go of Luna and got to his knees. Time to face the music. He was just about to rise when he felt Hunter grab him from behind. A hairy forearm wrapped around his neck, dragging him up against the other man's body. As they stood together, the cold steel muzzle of Hunter's weapon was pressed into his temple.

"Hunter," Luna begged with tears in her voice. "You said Gears could leave."

"Yeah," Mac drawled lazily. "We're all leaving. Listen to your girlfriend. Let go of Gears before I kill you."

Gears noticed that Mac said "before I kill you", not "then I won't kill you". Mac had evidently made up his mind about this situation. Gears' eyes popped to his left. Karma's gun was aimed at Hunter's back. If she took the shot, the round could go through Hunter and into him. Mac held his gun steady. His best friend was a good shot. He might get Hunter in the head, but he wasn't sure. Luna took in a sharp breath, and more tears gathered on her lashes. This was her brother. She didn't want to see him hurt. It was up to Gears to come up with something. He would just explain to Mac. They were friends, after all. He needed to make sure this didn't escalate any more.

Archer's cry drew everyone's attention. The baby had chosen this moment to awake screaming. A dark smile briefly crossed Mac's face. Gears saw the quirk of his lips before the look was gone. He knew what that smile meant. There was no way Gears was going to let Mac use a baby in a standoff. Especially when it was *his* baby.

"Who's this?" Mac dropped his gun and grabbed Luna by the hair. Her head was thrown back, and Mac easily plucked the baby out of her arms.

Rage that someone might hurt his son overwhelmed him. His reserve of understanding and patience flew off like a startled bird.

"Give me my son right now, Mac, or I'll fucking kill you." Gears elbowed Luna's brother in the stomach, then wrenched away from Hunter with strength he didn't know he possessed. Hunter bent over. Gears crossed in front of Luna. Mac froze in shock at his outburst. His friend let go of Archer as soon as Gears had his hands around the baby. He pulled the child from Mac's hands and cooed at the crying babe. He rocked him back and forth like he had seen Hunter do earlier.

Mac was still looking at him with a stunned expression on his face.

"No!" Luna screamed.

Gears spun around. Hunter had raised his gun. The pistol was aimed right at Gears and Archer. Without thought, Gears turned his body to protect Archer. If he was going to get shot, then fine, but no one would hurt his baby.

The sound of a single shot filled the air. Gears squeezed his eyes shut. His heart beat, once, twice. He opened his eyes then glanced around.

Karma was holding her cooling pistol as she stood in the shadow of the doorway. Hunter was on the floor. Blood was soaking into the carpet. Karma silently glided closer to The Original member.

Hunter still clutched his gun. He wheezed. This was crazy. Hunter might be his enemy, but he was also his child's uncle.

"Ah, hell." Gears grabbed Luna. "Save your brother." He glared at Mac. "Stand down." He then rushed to where Karma stood. "Holster that."

Mac took a hasty step back when Gears yelled at him. His friend's eyebrows went straight up into his hair. Karma put her sidearm away and held up her hands in a gesture of peace. When her hands were free, Gears handed Archer over to her.

"This is my son, Archer." He held Archer out. She nodded. "You any good with stopping a baby from crying?"

Karmas eyes softened. "I have a little practice."

"Good." Gears turned to Luna, but she wasn't touching Hunter. She was simply kneeling next to him with her hands around her waist. Hunter wheezed again.

Gears sank to the floor next to Luna's brother and took the gun from his hand.

"Luna, save your brother" he repeated.

"No." She wrapped her arms around her middle even tighter. Tears glistened in her eyes. "I can't." A single sob escaped her.

"Then I will." Gears tipped her brother on his side. The bullet had entered through one side of Hunter's back then exited through his chest. The round had probably punctured a lung. Gears also guessed it might have crashed through a rib as well. He moved Hunter to one side so that the damaged lung would fill with fluids and the healthy one wouldn't. He needed supplies.

Gears began to review past injuries he'd worked on that were similar, items he would need, and where he might find said items, but Luna's hand on his arm pulled him out of his thoughts.

"Let my brother die."

Gears shook his head slowly. She didn't mean that. Luna was angry right now, and hurt. He understood that, but one day she would regret this. He wouldn't let her live with the guilt. He would find the forgiveness he needed to save Hunter even if she couldn't.

"No. I'm a healer. It's in my blood." He took her hand. "Just like it's in you. Don't let him die because you're angry at him. That's not a reason." Luna took a shaky breath. "Conpar," Gears spoke evenly. "We're healers, not killers."

"Since he's my brother, it's easier if I heal him." She let go of Gears' hand and scooted closer to Hunter. She closed her eyes, then shoved Hunter's bloody shirt up. Setting her hands on her brother, Luna curled her body forward. Gears could hear her whispering to Hunter's skin. A few men were looking into the doorway, and Mac's eyes jumped around the room. Karma started to pace. She gently bounced Archer up and down and the baby giggled happily.

Gears had no idea if he sat next to Luna and Hunter for hours or minutes. Finally, she let go of her brother and faced him.

"Out beyond the ideas of right-doing and wrong-doing is a field." Luna's eyes glistened with unshed tears.

"I'll meet you there." Gears finished the Rumi quote, then drew her into his arms. He held her for a moment before he heard Hunter scramble to his feet.

"Luna—" Hunter began.

"No," she snapped at her brother as she climbed to her feet. "I don't want to hear what you have to say. You were honorable once, Hunter. I trusted your word."

"You have my word," Hunter growled at his sister.

"They all leave. All of them. Safely." She inclined her head at Mac.

Hunter's eyes flashed to Mac. "They all leave," Hunter repeated. "Safely."

Mac and Hunter stared at each other for a second. A silent discussion was clearly being passed between the two adversaries.

Gears got up from the floor and pulled Luna into his arms again. He kissed her lips softly.

"You're free to come with us, Luna." Mac glared at Hunter. "I assume Gears is here for you as well as his child. At least, I got that from the camera footage."

Luna shook her head sadly. "Thank you for the offer, but I made a deal. Archer is safe with his father at H.S.P.C., and I stay here with my brother."

It felt like someone was stabbing his heart. Gears raised his hand to feather along her neck.

"I can't live without you." He tipped his head forward and pressed it to hers. "I died before."

"You can live just fine. Before, when you died, that was an accident. You'll be healthy now." She smiled. "You'll be healthy, and I'll be happy knowing you're safe with Archer."

"I won't be happy knowing you're here. How will I know you're safe?"

"Hunter won't let anything happen to me, and I can write to you like before."

"What?" Mac glared at Gears. "Were you trading messages with The Originals?" His friend crossed his arms over his chest.

"Seriously, Luna?" Hunter growled. "You were sending notes to the H.S.P.C.?"

Gears didn't answer either man. He kept staring into Luna's blue eyes. "I want to hear from you to know you're alright. I don't trust Hunter." Gears placed a hand on her cheek. "Will I ever see you again?"

"We're a perfect match. We'll always meet at some time and some place. I love you."

Gears eyes prickled. A flood of emotions filled him, and he let them rise. The hurt, the pain, he felt them deeply, and because of his Luna, he let them have a place inside his heart. He didn't want to say goodbye, but she wasn't going to change her mind. He accepted her choice. He'd been trying to get her to come home with him for the entire trip, and nothing had swayed her. She felt an allegiance to her brother and The Originals. Honestly, he even understood that loyalty, and he appreciated that she was an honorable woman. He had the same commitment to Mac and the H.S.P.C. They really were Romeo and Juliet. They were just going to live at the end of their story. He wasn't sure if living without her was better than dying.

"I wish I had my backpack," he sighed.

"I got it." Brice appeared in the doorway. He held up one of Gears' backpacks that they must have brought from Headquarters. Gears crossed over to the sack and unzipped it. After a few seconds, he found what he was looking for. He pulled out his label maker and began to type. As he walked back over to face Luna, he printed out the little white label he'd just created.

The tag read, in simple black letters: LUNA'S MAN. Gears ripped off the tag and then pressed the adhesive strip to the back of his hand.

"I'm always going to be waiting to see you again."

"Rumi says 'Life is a balance between holding on…'" She paused to push away some tears from her eyes.

"And letting go." Gears kissed her, praying it wasn't the last time.

Chapter 16

"If light is in your heart, you will find your way home." Rumi~

Gears strode down the hall of the H.S.P.C. Headquarters building while he read his monthly letter from Chen-Ning. After he flipped through a page and a half about how much Chen-Ning loved Gino and their new puppy, he found one sentence on Luna.

According to Spider's men, Luna and her brother were traveling again. Gears wished he knew where they were heading and why. In an earlier letter, Chen-Ning said it appeared that Hunter was looking for something when they first left Monclova. His friend didn't know what they were searching for, though. Gears wondered if Chen-Ning was just speculating, or if he knew some detail he wasn't telling him.

Gears frowned. If only Luna would send him a note, anything. She had sent him zero messages, and he was going crazy with worry. No amount of exercise and Snow Flu research kept his mind off her. The only thing he knew was that Luna and her brother had been moving from place to place. Spider's men had tracked them. Gino and Chen-Ning sent him information as often as they could.

The stairs were up ahead. Gears passed the elevators, then opened the door to the main stairwell. Mac and Karma had been visiting for a few days, and he thought he would say goodbye.

Since he had begun lifting weights and jogging every day the stairs were his new favorite thing. He jogged down them. When he'd reached the fourth-floor landing, he heard a door slam above him.

"Gears!" He heard yelling behind him. Gears stopped and turned around.

Brice was hurrying down the steps. When he reached his side, he didn't stop but grabbed his arm and dragged him down the next flight.

"What is it, Brice?"

"You'll never believe it. Hunter is here with a few of The Originals," Brice said as they hit the next landing and then headed down more steps. "Luna is dying."

Gears flew after Brice. The two men hit the first floor, then threw open the door that let out into the hallway. Gears switched to a full sprint down the normally busy hall. He noted there were few people around. That must mean every available agent and guard-in-training was on lookout with The Originals here.

The hall opened out into a high-ceilinged foyer that was the main entrance to HQ. Ahead of him were two sets of huge bulletproof glass double doors. Gears skidded to a stop for a second.

Hunter was kneeling in the middle of the stone tiles with his hands resting on top of his hair. His head was bowed subserviently and his chin reached his chest. Gears spotted him first. A cot with missing legs was on the floor next to him. On the canvas top it looked like a dead woman was covered in a light blanket. Gears counted about forty-five men all aiming guns at Hunter. Mac was standing in the middle of the room facing Luna's brother.

Gears blew past Mac. He made it past his friend when Mac snagged his arm and hauled him backward.

"This could be a trap. She could have a grenade under her. When you touch her—"

"Are you going to make me swear at you again?" Gears shoved off his friend's hand.

"No." Mac let go.

Gears slowed his pace and moved a little more cautiously, but he still advanced. Hunter looked up from the floor as he approached, but he didn't move. Gears came around to the side of the cot. Luna looked gray. Her hair was stringy and lackluster. He couldn't even tell if she was breathing. He knelt down and checked for a pulse. He could feel a faint one. His eyes slashed to Hunter.

"I didn't do anything to her, I swear it." Hunter whispered to him, but his voice was clear in the open chamber. "She kept getting worse. I looked for doctors to help her, and medications. I've been everywhere and seen everyone. I don't know what to do. She's going to die. You were the only one I thought maybe…"

"She isn't going to die." Gears said the sentence as a demand. His voice echoed off the walls. "I'm a brilliant scientist and a doctor." He pushed the blanket away from her body so he could put his hands under her legs and shoulders. She was so light. It was like picking up a cloud. He lifted her easily and pressed her closer to his body. "You should've brought her to me first," he added.

The minute his hands pressed around her slim shoulders and his arm sealed against her skin, he felt dizzy. Dizziness wasn't a feeling he had experienced for months. His arm and hands tingled and he closed his eyes.

"Are you okay?" Mac asked. He felt Mac's hand on his shoulder steadying him.

He nodded, then looked down. Luna was staring up at him. Her blue eyes were not as bright, but they were just as beautiful as he recalled.

"Gears," she slurred. "I don't feel so good."

"Luna?" Hunter's head lifted. "Fuck me, she hasn't spoken in weeks."

"I need my healer," she whispered as her hand raised and wrapped around his neck.

Electrical currents felt like they were being drained from him. Heat began to spread in his middle than work toward his crotch. He hadn't thought about sex in months, but his dick seemed to have decided that intercourse was the most important topic at the moment.

Luna lifted her head to kiss his lips slowly. He got drawn into her mouth instantly. He couldn't help it. He sucked and licked at the soft interior of her lips and forgot where he was.

"Gears?" Mac's voice cut through the sexual fog that he was being dragged into.

"Hum?" He lifted his eyes and saw that Mac was shaking his head.

"What are you doing?" Mac glanced around the room. "She's sick."

"And I'm the only one who is going to make her better." Gears looked from Mac to Hunter still kneeling on the floor. "Listen, I don't fully understand why Luna and I are connected. I might never figure out the mystery." He paused. "That's absurd, I will figure it out one day, but for now I have an educated guess that without Luna I might die." He looked to Mac. "And without me, Luna might die. We need to share energy."

"Share energy?" Hunter asked.

"Exchange it." He nuzzled her cheek and Luna sighed. "Intimately."

"Intimately?" Hunter glared. "You're not touching my sister ever again." Hunter popped to his feet aggressively. Four men yelled for him to get down. Mac raised his rifle.

Hunter swore, then dropped to his knees again while he placed his hands back on top of his head.

"I can't help that I need her and she needs me." Gears adjusted her in his arms. "Look at her, Hunter. You're her brother. Don't you care about her?"

Hunter's head angled up to scan Luna's dull, gray, lifeless form. He nodded.

"Mac." Gears started to walk with Luna in his arms.

"Are you in your boss mode now?" Mac followed him. "I think I'm getting used to it."

"Yes, I am." Gears reached the archway that led into the hall, then stopped. "I want you and Hunter to work out some kind of deal."

"No deals with The Originals."

"Figure it out, because Luna and I have to see each other to be able to live. Either you and Hunter can pick one of us to live or you're going to have to make a deal."

"Damn." Mac put his hand on his arm when Gears tried to start heading over to the elevators. "Wait, while I'm doing that, what're you going to be doing?"

"While you work out the logistics, I will be in my bedroom with Luna." He grinned. "Exchanging energy."

"Yuck." Mac let go of his arm and spun around. He barked out for the men to stand down. "Come on, Hunter. We have to cooperate."

"Fuck that," Hunter responded.

"I agree, but it's either we make a deal or we kill them," he heard Mac say as the elevator doors closed. "Which is it? I don't have all day."

Gears leaned against the wall and took the first relaxed breath he'd taken since leaving Luna. She was here with him again. His boy was safe and he had her in his arms once more. When they got to his room, he could touch her again, taste her, love her.

His heart pounded, but this time with excitement.

"Your heart is pounding," Luna murmured as she snuggled closer to him. Gears smiled.

"That's because it beats for you."

Epilogue

"I once had a thousand desires. But in my one
desire to know you—all else melted away."
Rumi~

When Gears was a child, he remembered Christmas. His parents would buy him a present and he would have to wait and wait. Then, on the morning of Christmas Day, he could open it and feel the joy of the gift he was given.

The same feeling of joy and excitement filled him as he waited at the gates of the Headquarters building for Luna.

The yelling and the extra ammo being passed around signified she was almost to the gate. He was starting to love the sound of safeties being switched to semi and the smell of gunpowder.

Men on the gun turrets on both sides of the large wall aimed at the approaching Original's vehicles. He pushed up his glasses. He hadn't seen her in a month. Every time she left, he hated it and his melancholy forced him to throw himself into his work with gusto to keep his loneliness at bay. But then before long, she came back as beautiful as ever and he could spend an entire month in her warm embrace. His heart picked up its beat as if the organ knew she was on the other side of the wall.

The huge thick metal door on his right opened with a soprano-pitched shriek. Gears followed four guards out of the H.S.P.C. compound and onto the road outside. They surrounded him as they waited for the variety of vehicles to halt.

Five trucks with mounted machine guns parked in a row. This was the first time Hunter had let such a small escort come to HQ. He hoped that fewer guards was a good sign.

Gears waited while three men climbed out of every vehicle and took positions aiming at the agents and sentinels up on the wall and around the gate. When everyone had a gun pointed at everyone else, the door to the third truck finally opened. Luna slipped out wearing a long white skirt and a pale blue shirt that matched her eyes. She floated like an angel, and just like always he forgot that they were encircled by enough guns to start a war.

"Your soul is lovely today. I missed you," he said as Luna slipped into his arms like she was made for him.

"Thank you." She kissed his mouth, and before he could remind himself not to kiss her in front of people, he was licking the inside of the delicious cavern. His hand went to the side of her chest and he began to tug at the bottom of her shirt. A blind person could probably see the bolts of lightning sparking between them.

"Yuck." Hunter's voice caught his attention. Both Mac and Hunter had picked up saying that a lot since he and Luna had begun to spend time together.

Gears' brain kicked on. When he was with Luna she stole every lucid thought he had. It didn't seem to matter how much time passed, but he could never slow his raging hormones when she was around. He pulled away from her to lessen the temptation to have sex right in front of all these men.

"Hunter," he muttered, pushing up his glasses.

Hunter was in the front seat, and unless Gears had Archer with him, he never got out.

Today he was changing it up. The door to his armored truck opened.

"I don't have Archer today," Gears explained to Hunter as the big man glanced down at him. "He has the sniffles and I put him to bed, but I'll bring him next time." Gears still wasn't a big fan of Luna's brother, but Hunter did have a soft spot for Archer that Gears couldn't ignore.

Gears had hoped that his explanation would have Hunter leaving so he could have Luna all to himself, but Hunter got out anyway.

After Luna's brother hopped down, he turned around to take a cardboard box from his driver. Luna stepped to the side as Hunter came to stand in front of him. After her brother paused, he opened the lid of the box.

In the container was a white and pink blanket. Archer didn't really need a blanket, but Gears supposed that if Hunter wanted to give his nephew the item it was fine with him. When Hunter extended the box further, Gears was forced to either take it or let it drop. He grabbed the outside and Hunter reached inside and pushed the blanket down. Under the fabric was a sleeping baby.

"What's going on?" he asked as soon as the child came into view.

Hunter shushed him, then dropped his voice lower.

"Mother claims this girl will one day destroy her," Hunter explained as he gave fugitive glances to the men still standing around.

"What?"

"The members have decided that she should be put to death," Hunter said quietly.

"What?"

Hunter shoulders dropped. "You say 'what' a lot."

"No, I don't." Gears pushed up his glasses, then looked to Luna. "Well, maybe sometimes I do. I just don't have this figured out yet."

"What's to figure out? You can either have the baby, hide it or something, or I can take it back and kill it." Hunter glanced around. "Your choice."

"He has a soft spot for children." Luna raised her eyebrows as if challenging her brother to deny it.

"Shut it, Luna," Hunter glared. "Take it or leave it."

Gears glanced around as well. No one seemed to be paying any attention to them. He had the feeling Hunter was taking a big risk bringing him the baby. He pushed up his glasses. He wasn't going to let The Originals randomly kill a baby because of a prophecy from a child they had made into a false prophet.

Gears held the box gently. "Goodbye, Hunter. I'll see you in a month." He turned to head into the building. "Come on, Luna."

"Bye, Hunter." Luna walked at his side while behind them Hunter climbed back into his truck without speaking. Gears didn't talk to anyone either. He simply entered the compound and started back toward the main building along the drive.

After Luna and he had strolled along the gravel for a few moments, he stopped and turned around. All the men were still targeting the departing convoy. None of them paid him and Luna any attention. Their inattentiveness fine with him.

Reaching into the box, Gears scooped the little baby out of the cardboard. Luna took the box from him and tucked it under her arm.

"She kind of looks like the devil," Luna commented. "And she cries a lot, then she's happy for a while, then she switches again. She gave a few of the women a headache."

Gears stared down at the baby. "She doesn't look like the devil." He glanced up at Luna. "What did her mom and dad say about killing her? Didn't they want her? Didn't they fight for her?"

Luna's forehead crinkled. "Her parents wanted her to be killed. Mother insisted. It caused a big argument because Hunter is the leader and he didn't agree. I stayed out of it because I'm already a traitor for loving you. Plus,

I knew my brother wouldn't let anything happen to an innocent babe."

"I'm glad Hunter didn't let them kill her." He cradled the child as they reached the front steps.

"Mother got angry and left when the baby wasn't killed right then and there. No one knows where she ran off to. The members said we had to kill the baby to get Mother to return to us. Hunter did a big show and pretended to murder the baby. He lit the body on fire so no one would find out he was lying. I told him to bring her to you. I knew my match would know what to do. You're brilliant, even if you do ask 'what' all the time."

Gears kissed the baby's cheek. "I'll figure this out."

"I know," Luna laughed. "My perfect match is brilliant and a great healer, just like me."

"I guess we have two children now." A warm feeling spread deep within his soul at Luna's unshakable belief in him. Gears looked down at the baby. "I have two kids, a woman who loves my soul, work that gives me pride, and a beating heart. Thank you, Luna."

Luna tipped her head and leaned on his shoulder. "Romeo and Juliet never had it so good."

The baby began to fuss, and Gears rocked her in his arms as he walked into Headquarters.

Just when they stepped up to enter the building, the child opened her eyes and looked up at him. The baby was staring up at him with blood red eyes.

"She *does* kind of look like the devil."

~ The End ~

Next in the series:

2:05 a.m.

The Ice Era Chronicles (Book 2)

http://mybook.to/205am

Locked in an abandoned cage with no memory, Arrow's life seemed to be crumbling like the building around him. Little did he know his red eyed angel would lead him to freedom. Rescuing his mind, body, and soul.

Nova is content with her life as Gears' research assistant, but when mankind's survival is on the line she risks her sanity to complete an unsanctioned mission. Without the doctor's knowledge, she must traverse the Northern Earth Dens to find the rumor that may be the answer to the survival of the human race.

Get your copy of 2:05 a.m.

http://mybook.to/205am

Thank you for reading

Grinding My Gears

If you enjoyed this book and would like to give back to the author, please consider writing a review! Reviews are a tremendous help for authors. So if you were moved and enjoyed this book enough to write even one sentence of encouragement it would be a huge boon.

https://www.goodreads.com/review/new/35482200-grinding-my-gears

Want more of the Ice Era Chronicles? Get a FREE story! Join C.M.Moore's exclusive readers group for a free story, GIVEAWAYS, Advanced reader opportunities and Pre-order notifications!

Join at:

http://eepurl.com/dnoLrr

Other books by C.M.Moore:

<u>Ice Era Chronicles</u>

1:05 a.m.

2:05 a.m.

<u>Off-the-Rails Ice Era Chronicles</u>

Raiden Out the Storm

Two for Tea

Find out when the next book comes out!
Connect with C.M.Moore:

Facebook:
https://www.facebook.com/profile.php?id=10001044
2116825

Goodreads:
https://www.goodreads.com/author/show/7397933.
C_M_Moore

Pinterest:
https://www.pinterest.com/cmmooreauthor/

Website:
http://www.authorcmmoore.com/

There will be at least 12 novels in the ICE ERA CHRONICLES and 10 novellas in the OFF-THE-RAILS ICE ERA CHRONICLES. Want more time in the snow? Get a FREE Novella! Join the exclusive readers group for

GIVEAWAYS, Advanced reader opportunities and Pre-order notifications!

Join us:

http://eepurl.com/dnoLrr

Check out the AUTHOR WEBSITE:

www.authorcmmoore.com

www.ingramcontent.com/pod-product-compliance
Lightning Source LLC
Chambersburg PA
CBHW021958170626
46808CB00001B/208